"Step on up, cowboy. I promise not to bite," Dory said

She winked exaggeratedly at the men, who were lapping up her antics like thirsty dogs at the trough, rather than the kissing booth.

"Looks as if you're doing just fine without my business," Clint replied, caught off guard by the realization that he wanted to kiss her. Not a token peck in front of the crowd, but one of those slow wet kisses that made his blood simmer.

The knowledge shook him. When had he started thinking of Dory in those terms?

"Chicken," she taunted, her glittering eyes locked with his as she plucked the tickets from the hand of her next customer.

Clint smiled. Oh, he planned on kissing her, all right. Later. Without an audience.

In fact, if she was willing, he planned on doing a whole lot more than kissing.

Blaze

Dear Reader,

These past two years have been a time for me to flex my writing skills. I've contributed to an anthology with two other authors, written two time travels and this ENCOUNTERS story. Of all the departures from my usual path, I had anticipated that the ENCOUNTERS would have been the easiest. Not so.

What a roller-coaster ride *Texas Heat* was for me to write. I love ranch settings and fish-out-of-water stories, so no problems there. I've written in short format before, so again, no problem with that. The characters themselves are the ones who gave me trouble. It was too hard to let them go.

As different as heroines Dory, Lisa and Jessica are, I totally adored each one from the start. I thought they found the perfect heroes, and I wanted to stay with them on their journeys. And soon you'll meet Kate Manning again...I'm plotting her story now, and since she's best friends with Dory, Lisa and Jessica, I think I just may have to find out what the ladies are up to. Well, time to get back to work.

Enjoy!

Debbi Rawlins

Debbi Rawlins

TEXAS HEAT

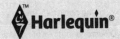

TORONTO NEW YORK LONDON
AMSTERDAM PARIS SYDNEY HAMBURG
STOCKHOLM ATHENS TOKYO MILAN MADRID
PRAGUE WARSAW BUDAPEST AUCKLAND

Recycling programs
for this product may
not exist in your area.

ISBN-13: 978-0-373-36551-7

TEXAS HEAT

Copyright © 2009 by Debbi Quattrone

www.Harlequin.com

Printed in U.S.A.

ABOUT THE AUTHOR

Debbi Rawlins lives in central Utah, out in the country, surrounded by woods and deer and wild turkeys. It's quite a change for a city girl, who didn't even know where the state of Utah was until four years ago. Of course, unfamiliarity never stopped her. Between her junior and senior years of college she spontaneously left home in Hawaii and bummed around Europe for five weeks by herself. And much to her parents' delight, she returned home with only a quarter in her wallet.

Books by Debbi Rawlins

Prologue

"I THINK THEY'RE HERE," Maria, the Manning's longtime housekeeper said as she stopped squeezing lemons and squinted into the sun streaming in through the window.

Excited to see her college friends, Kate Manning yanked off her apron and started out of the large crowded kitchen when she remembered her engagement ring sitting on the windowsill over the sink. She grabbed the one-karat diamond solitaire and smiled wryly at Maria, when the older woman shook her graying head in mock disapproval.

Kate had accepted the ring from her boyfriend of two years a month ago and had already misplaced it three times. No doubt a psychologist would have a field day with that information. Lately, Kate had been wondering herself what lay beneath the uncharacteristic absentmindedness. But not now. She didn't have time to think about anything but the weekend's festivities. Here at the Sugarloaf, her family's ranch, the Fourth of July celebration was a Manning tradition that included neighboring ranches for fifty miles.

She slid the ring onto her finger as she hurried through the sprawling ranch house to fling open the front door. The black Town Car she'd sent to the Houston airport for her friends pulled into the circular driveway and stopped several feet from the wraparound porch.

Lisa Stevens stepped out of the car first, blond, beautiful, perfect figure, gorgeous hair, flawless skin…she hadn't changed a bit since college. Or maybe Kate didn't notice a difference because Lisa was the only one she'd seen since they'd graduated five years ago. A successful Chicago reporter, Lisa had tracked a lead to Dallas, and Kate had met her there for a night out. Naturally, Lisa had gotten her story. The woman could charm the fangs off a rattlesnake.

Dory Richards was right behind her, a direct contrast in torn, faded jeans, a baggy dark T-shirt and black running shoes. She looked as if she hadn't brushed her long brown hair in a week, but then she'd always looked that way. A perpetual tomboy, even the few times she'd dated in college, Dory had never bothered with makeup or the latest clothing styles.

From the other side of the car, Jessica Mead rounded the hood of the car. Kate almost didn't recognize her. The woman had totally transformed herself. Oozing sophistication and glamour, her hair was pulled into a fashionable French twist and her tailored sleeveless linen dress obviously hadn't come off the rack. Absurdly high heels made her a good five inches taller than her college days of scruffy jeans and tennis shoes.

"Kate!" Dory noticed her first, rushing to her and nearly knocking her over in her enthusiasm. "You cut your hair."

"Gosh, I did that over two years ago. I can't believe it's been five years. We swore we'd never let that much time go by."

Lisa and Jessica joined them in a group hug, and then they dragged their luggage from the trunk of the car into the foyer. Lisa had a medium bag, Dory a small one, but Jessica looked as if she'd packed for a week.

"Very nice," Lisa said, ducking her head to scan the formal living room off to the right. "Not exactly how I pictured a ranch house."

Kate chuckled. "We never go in there. My mom insisted that we keep one room pristine for unexpected company." Her parents had been gone for thirteen years now, but neither she nor her brothers had the heart to swap out the stuffy, impractical furniture. "Now, the rest of the house…well…just remember I have two brothers who live here."

"Come on. Let's see it." Jessica held out her hand, and when Kate gave her a puzzled frown, Jessica sighed. "The ring, sweetie, show us the ring."

"Oh." Kate promptly held out her hand and wiggled her fingers, making the diamond sparkle.

"Wow, nice rock. They must pay school principals pretty damn well around here." Lisa gave her a low five.

"I'll say." Jessica smiled. "He's got my approval already."

Dory teasingly rolled her eyes. "You're so easy."

"We are so not going there," Lisa said, and everyone laughed, and then Jessica tried unsuccessfully to stifle a yawn.

"Sorry," she murmured. "I've been working a lot lately."

"You're always working." Lisa checked her watch. "What's local time?"

Jessica looked at her in annoyed disbelief. "Look who's talking."

Dory shook her head. "Oh, here we go."

"You guys must all be exhausted," Kate cut in, still the peacemaker of the group. "The ninety-minute drive from Houston is bad enough, especially after a long plane ride." She picked up one of Jessica's bags. "Let me show you to your rooms. Take your time freshening up and then we'll have some iced tea and talk."

Impulsively, she set the bag back down and opened her arms for another group hug. It really was good to see them all together. Surely that was the reason for the emotion welling up inside of her. And nothing to do with misgivings.

THE WILD, WILD WEST

1

TWO DAYS AGO Dory Richards had been swatting at mosquitoes in the humid jungles of Cambodia. Today she was in hot, dry West Texas. Good thing she slept well on planes. With all the traveling she'd been doing for the past three years, she'd quickly learned how to cheat jet lag.

Anxious to make the most of her long weekend, she didn't bother unpacking her suitcase. So her clothes would be a bit wrinkled. It wasn't as if she'd stoop to ironing them. Besides, she'd brought only jeans and T-shirts and two denim blouses. This was a ranch, after all, and she couldn't imagine people getting too dressed up for the Fourth of July festivities.

She'd almost made it out of the guest room she'd been assigned when she caught a glimpse of her hair in the dresser mirror. The scary mess stopped her, and she conceded to dragging a brush through the long unruly strands before gathering the whole thing into a sloppy ponytail.

As soon as she stepped into the hall she heard kitchen noises and followed the clang of pots and pans, and a stream of excited Spanish. She found her friend Kate in the middle of the chaos, an apron around her slender waist and a wooden spoon in one hand as she rattled on in Spanish to a young olive-skinned woman kneading dough at the island counter.

Three other women were in the large modern kitchen, one busy at the stainless steel stove, stirring something in a huge pot, and the other two shucking corn. They looked up, smiled at her and kept working.

"Need another pair of hands?" Dory asked.

Kate spun around, her mouth twisting wryly. "I just might have to take you up on that." She set down the spoon on the mauve-and-cream granite countertop and reached around to loosen her apron. "I'd really hoped to be more organized before you and Lisa and Jessica arrived so that we could visit more."

Dory stopped her. "Hey, don't worry about us. I'm ready to roll up my sleeves."

Kate shook her head. "I'm usually so much better at this. I should be. Our family has only hosted the event for fifty years now." She sighed. "I've been too distracted."

"Gee, I can't imagine why." Dory grinned. "I can't believe you're gonna get married in six months."

"Me, neither." The fleeting look of panic on Kate's face startled Dory. Kate slid a glance at the shorter, plump woman standing at the sink, suds up to her elbows and eyeing Kate with troubled black eyes. Kate smiled brightly and shrugged. "I *had* to do something to get us all together. Dory, this is Maria. She's been with our family forever."

They exchanged pleasantries, and then the woman went back to work and Dory studied Kate, wondering what the heck was going on. A couple of weeks ago Kate had called the gang, excited as all get out over her engagement. But something was wrong. "I can't believe we let five years go by," Dory said, frustrated. With a kitchen full of ears, now wasn't the time for Dory to voice her concern. "Give me something to do," she said. "Maybe later we'll have time to talk."

Kate's eyebrows went up in amusement. "You ever learn how to cook?"

"Ah, well…there's gotta be something else I can—"

The back door opened and everyone turned to look at the tall, broad-shouldered man who walked in, promptly removed his Stetson and shoved a hand through his longish dark hair. Well over six feet, he wore snug jeans, cowboy boots and a killer smile. "Morning, ladies."

The young woman kneading dough blushed to the roots of her raven hair.

"Clint Manning, you better have wiped off your boots, or so help me—"

"Now, Katie, would I mess up your kitchen?" He looked past Kate and winked at Dory. "You must be one of my sister's college friends she's been all fired up to see."

Dory didn't miss the way he'd sized her up. Obviously he didn't remember her. They'd met briefly back East at the graduation ceremony. Though Dory wasn't the type of woman men usually did remember, a fact that didn't bother her any. He, on the other hand, wasn't a man many women forgot, no matter how short the meeting, and she suspected he knew it.

She moved toward him, her hand out. "Dory Richards," she said, pumping his hand with too much enthusiasm, a bad habit that her boss had twice suggested she work on.

Surprise flickered in his green eyes, and then his mouth curved in a devilish smile. "I like a woman with a firm grip," he said, and then exaggeratedly flexed his hand.

Kate swatted him with the apron she'd removed from around her waist. "You guys met at graduation, remember?"

"Did we?" Dory smiled innocently.

"Yeah, that's right." Clint nodded, clearly lying. "Nice to see you again." He looked back at Kate as he opened the stainless steel refrigerator door. "What's for lunch? I'm starving."

"Lunch?" Kate glared at him. "Does it look as if we have time to make lunch?"

He frowned at her. "Hey, I'm not asking anyone to wait on me. I just figured this might be my last chance before the boys from the Double R get here with—"

"Oh, my God." Kate covered her mouth with her hand and briefly closed her eyes.

"What?"

Kate squinted bleakly at her brother. "You're going to kill me."

"You did remember to order the lumber, right?" He rubbed his right temple, looking as if he already knew he wouldn't like her answer.

She glanced at the round wall clock over the stove. "You still have time to pick it up. Take the trailer."

Clint groaned. "That's over a two-hour round trip, and that's not counting loading."

"I'm sorry. Dory will go with you." Kate met her eyes, and Dory nodded. "She can help."

"That's a lot of lumber. I'm not taking a girl—" Clint pressed his lips together, his gaze fixed on his sister.

Dory grinned. "Yes?"

He slid her a guilty glance, and then grabbed an apple from a fruit bowl on the counter. "I'll rustle up one of the boys from the back pasture to go with me."

Kate sighed. "They're all busy and we really don't have time."

Dory plucked a ripened pear from the bowl. "Come on, cowboy, I'll try not to show you up."

CLINT TOOK HIS OWN TRUCK, knowing he'd have to use the extended bed. After checking the trailer in the rearview mirror, he pulled out of the private dirt road that led to the family ranch and onto the highway. Beside him on the bench seat, Dory stretched out her long, jean-clad legs and munched her pear. Above her knee the faded denim was torn, matching another tear he'd noticed below her rear pocket. Nothing to do with making a fashion statement, that was for sure. Even her right hem was frayed where it skimmed a battered tennis shoe.

No, she wasn't afraid of getting her hands dirty, he'd have to admit. She'd jumped right in to help hook up the trailer, and loaded the ramps and straps by herself. She hadn't even waited for him to toss her a pair of gloves. Still, he felt weird letting a woman do physical work beside him. His sister was no flower herself, but even Kate stuck to her duties in the house.

"What's the lumber we're picking up for?" Dory asked, using the back of her wrist to wipe pear juice from the corner of her mouth. Her ponytail had loosened and her hair was all over the place.

Clint smiled at her lack of self-consciousness. "Tomorrow's game booths."

"Game booths? Like what?"

"The usual…tic-tac-toe, ring toss, that sort of thing."

"Kind of like a carnival."

"Yeah, I suppose."

"We have a traveling carnival in Hawaii, but I haven't been in years."

Surprised, he looked over at her. "That's where you're from?"

"Yep, born and raised. My parents moved there during the free-love sixties era from Kansas. We lived in a commune until I was about thirteen."

"You're serious?"

She shrugged. "It's not much different than you and Kate and your brother living here on the ranch all your life."

He saw a major difference but no point in arguing. "How did you end up at a college on the East Coast?"

"A friend from high school talked me into it. I almost transferred out because I hated the snow. How about you?"

"I didn't go far. University of Houston for four years. I liked coming home on weekends and working on the ranch with my brother, Joe."

She shifted, bending one leg so that she faced him. "What did you study?"

"Business, believe it or not."

"That is a surprise."

Clint shrugged. "It's not like I wanted to work in an office. I figured I might learn something that would make the ranch more efficient."

"Did you?"

He gritted his teeth, annoyed that she was probing areas better left alone. "Yep."

"So what kind of changes did you make?"

"Why all the questions? You writing a book?"

At his terse tone, she stiffened. "Jeez Louise, I thought we were making small talk, passing the time, being friendly." She sniffed and twisted around to face the road again. "We don't have to talk. We could listen to the radio if you want. Or I could sing to you. But I warn you, I can't carry a tune worth a damn."

He exhaled loudly. "Sorry, it's kind of a touchy subject." He felt the weight of her stare but she didn't comment, which oddly encouraged him to add, "My brother, Joe, he wasn't interested in making any changes."

"Ah. He's the oldest, right?"

Keeping his eyes on the road, Clint nodded. "He pretty much took over the ranch after our parents died. Kate was only fourteen and I was going into my senior year in high school."

"He couldn't have been much older himself."

"He'd just finished his sophomore year at UCLA."

"Wow!"

That was all Clint had to say on the subject. He knew he owed Joe a lot. It hadn't been easy for him to drop out of school, take on the ranch and two resentful teenagers. Neither Kate nor Clint would've made it to college if it weren't for Joe. But sometimes it was hard for Clint to keep his mouth shut when it came to the old-school way the ranch was still run. "So what do you do?"

"I'm a forensic anthropologist."

He waited until he'd safely passed a horse trailer parked on the shoulder of the highway and then glanced her way. She was tightening her ponytail and with her arms raised, her T-shirt clung to her breasts. Odd he hadn't noticed before how full and round they were. "I'm not sure what that means."

"I study remains mostly."

"Like bones?"

She chuckled. "Yeah, like bones."

"Man, that would creep me out."

"Wimp."

He grunted but ignored her teasing. Figured she had a job like that. "So what? You work with law enforcement?"

"Actually, I've spent the last six months in Vietnam and Cambodia, identifying remains of missing soldiers." The teasing tone was gone. Her voice had softened. "It's so sad that families have had to wait this long to find out what happened to their missing loved ones from the war."

"That's true, all right," he agreed quietly. "They're lucky they have people like you to finally give them some closure."

"Yeah, well, the findings are always kind of bitter-sweet, you know?"

"I can imagine." His gaze went to her hands. Her nails were uneven but clean, the skin badly scraped on two of her knuckles. He understood now why she wasn't like Kate's other two friends. They seemed like nice enough women, pretty, well put together, his type actually. Stupid when he stopped to think about it, but the high maintenance ones were the kind that attracted him. Maybe that's why he'd never entertained the thought of marriage. Too damn much work.

"Hey, look." She straightened and pointed to an eagle soaring low against the cloudless blue sky. "Beautiful, isn't he?"

Clint slowed down so he could appreciate the grace of the bird, and grinned. "How do you know it's a he?"

"Guys have to try harder to attract a mate. That's why males in most species have all the stunning feathers and bright colors," she said matter-of-factly. "When it's time to mate, girls just have to show up."

He chuckled. She did have a point.

2

DORY WAS SURPRISED when they turned down a dirt road under an arching sign that announced the Double R Ranch. It had seemed more like twenty minutes instead of an hour since they'd left the Manning's place, which was quite a spread as it turned out… about two thousand acres. Mostly flat pastureland, much of it fenced off for grazing cattle. For the entire ride, that pretty much had been all there was to see, more grazing land. Although she hadn't focused on the scenery half as much as she had the man sitting beside her.

She liked watching his hands as they confidently gripped the wheel. They were large and tanned, the back of his fingers sprinkled sparingly with crisp dark hair. Rolled-back sleeves exposed broad, big-boned wrists and muscled forearms, and his blue cotton shirt did nothing to hide his well-formed biceps.

He obviously hadn't shaved in a couple of days, and she wondered if that omission had been deliberate. Had he tried for that perfect, rugged, cowboy look? No, he seemed like a man who enjoyed the outdoors and wasn't afraid to sweat. Sure, she worked with a lot of big, muscular guys like that on digs, but unlike them, Clint had a lithe grace that had caught her attention earlier when he hooked up the trailer.

Weird, because she wasn't normally attracted to a man based on physical attributes, even one as good-looking as Clint. In fact, she tended to ignore the head-turners. She figured they got enough female attention.

The road to the Double R had obviously once been graveled and graded but not well maintained, and the truck dipped and bounced for nearly a mile before a large white house and outbuildings came into view. Good thing. Her fanny had had enough, and that was saying something since she seemed to spend half her life in a Jeep lately.

"I hope some of the hands are close by to help load the lumber." Clint pulled the truck up to the front of the barn. "Kate was supposed to have called ahead."

"I don't see anybody."

"The Reynoldses own this place, but times have been kind of tough for them lately," he said grimly. "They lost a good deal of their herd to cattle rustlers last year and had to lay off half their men."

"Rustlers? You're kidding."

"Wish I was."

"That sounds like something out of the old west."

"Darlin', out here, it still is the old west at times." He opened his door. "That's why I told Joe that we've got to start looking at—" He cut himself off, shaking his head, and then slid out from behind the wheel.

Dory scrambled out on her side. "What did you tell him?"

"Doesn't matter."

"Of course it matters." At his annoyed expression, she shrugged a shoulder. "Look, I'm just curious. What was your idea?"

The way he set his jaw told her it was time to leave the subject alone. He picked up his hat, pushed a hand through his hair in obvious frustration, and then reset the Stetson on his head. "I'm gonna go check if anyone's in the barn."

She leaned a hip against the truck and watched him walk away, his strides long and purposeful. Was he in a hurry to get away from her probing questions? Or worried about getting the load of lumber back in time to start working on the game booths? Probably both, she thought, sighing.

It wasn't that she was being nosy. She didn't have brothers or sisters, and although she understood sibling dynamics on a textbook level, she lacked the human experience. She did know that Kate adored both of her brothers, and that the older one had become more a father figure over the years. But Clint was older than Kate, about thirty was Dory's guess, so he probably didn't appreciate the perception of being kept under Joe's thumb.

Still, Joe obviously knew what he was doing to keep a ranch that large profitable. Dory wisely kept the observation to herself.

She shaded her eyes and gazed around the Double R. The place was spread out with a barn, what looked like a bunkhouse, stables and a corral where three horses grazed. But, unlike the Manning's ranch, there was no buzz of activity. Then again, she knew some of the goings-on had to do with the big July Fourth get-together.

Clint emerged from the barn, solo, his expression grim, and she had a feeling they had a ton of work ahead of them. She didn't mind. She just hoped he had a spare pair of gloves. Getting dirty was one thing, but getting pricked by splinters was something else.

"The lumber is stacked behind the barn," he said,

shaking his head as he closed the distance between them. "But we're not gonna get much help loading. Part of their south fence came down last night in the wind and most of the men are rounding up strays."

"No problem. We should be able to handle it. But I'll need some gloves."

He pulled open the driver's door, eyeing her with amusement. "I deliver you back crippled and Kate will take a branding iron to me."

"Oh, please." Dory tightened her ponytail, preparing for the work ahead. She might be useless in the kitchen, but out here…this was her world. "I bet I load as many boards as you do."

One side of his mouth hiked up. "Get in. We'll drive around to the back."

She did as he asked, smug in the knowledge that she was going to surprise the heck out of him. She was in better shape than she looked. Often she'd hiked uphill for miles to get to a dig site, and then spent another two hours with shovel in hand. Loading lumber would be a vacation.

"Check the glove box," Clint said as he steered the truck around the barn. "There might be some in there. If not, I might have a pair in my toolbox in the back."

She opened the compartment, which was jammed with the truck manual, a package of beef jerky, binoculars, a couple of maps and a small box of condoms. Quickly she slammed the door and stared straight ahead as they rounded the barn.

"Nothing, huh?" He pulled the truck to a stop. "If we don't find a pair, you can use mine."

"A callus or two won't kill me." She jerked on the door handle, anxious to jump out, annoyed with herself for being so flustered. So what if he kept condoms in his glove box? Good to know he was responsible. Although it didn't matter to her. Why should it?

"Wait a minute," he said, and slid an arm across the seat back behind her shoulders.

Her chest tightened as he slowly turned his face toward hers, his warm moist breath brushing the side of her jaw. She blinked, frozen, not knowing what to do, before finally giving in and meeting his eyes. He flashed her a grin and then twisted around to look out the rear window as he backed the truck and trailer toward the pile of lumber.

She let out a whoosh of air, and before he cut the engine, she jumped out of the truck, willing the heat that stung her cheeks to subside. Had she totally gone out of her mind? She seriously needed some rest. How could she actually have believed for a second that he'd been about to kiss her?

"You okay?" He'd gotten out and come around the back of the trailer to stare at her, his green gaze warm with concern.

"Fine." She looked away and nodded toward the daunting stacks of lumber. "That's it?"

Clint chuckled. "That's enough." He lowered the truck's tailgate, hopped up on the bed and went to a large metal toolbox anchored down behind the cab. After rooting around inside he produced a pair of tan leather gloves that he tossed to her.

She tried them on. They were too big but better than nothing.

He gathered the heavy-duty tie-down straps and bungee cords they'd brought and jumped off the bed. "I'm thinking I'll load and you should get up there and make sure the boards stay stacked until we can strap them down."

Dory smiled wryly, knowing that he was trying to keep her task light. "How about we both load and then worry about securing them?"

He studied her for a moment. "Hugh is the Reynoldses' foreman. He's the only one in the barn. If he sees you working, he's gonna want to come out and help. The guy turned seventy last month and has a bad back."

"Then quit talking and let's get this done before he sees me." She adjusted her gloves and tried to pick up four boards at once, but quickly found that her limit was three.

Clint mumbled something she couldn't hear, and then more clearly said, "You stick to the trailer, and I'll load the truck."

She didn't argue. With the trailer being lower to the ground it was easier for her to stack the boards and she'd be better able to keep up with his pace. On the negative side, given the distance between them, the capacity to ogle him as he worked was far greater. Unfortunately, she found the temptation hard to ignore with the way the worn denim of his jeans molded his leans hips and appealing backside.

Though after forty minutes working under the broiling afternoon sun, her thoughts pretty much narrowed to finishing the job. She was tired and thirsty and only sheer stubbornness drove her to keep picking up boards and swinging them onto the trailer. The steady rhythm she'd engaged was hypnotic, and when Clint called out for her to take a break, he startled her. She spun toward his voice, the movement dizzyingly fast, and she felt her body sway.

"Hey, you okay?"

"Yep, fine." She grabbed the trailer railing for support.

He pulled off his gloves and got them each a bottle of water from the truck's cab. "Here."

"Thanks." She fumbled with the cap and then greedily downed two large gulps so fast that it made her chest hurt.

"Take it easy," he said, touching her arm. "You shouldn't let yourself get that thirsty."

She nodded. "I know better." The warmth of his skin on hers did nothing to help clear her head, so she moved her arm away.

Confusion flickered in his gaze and he seemed about to say something when they heard the pounding of hooves coming in their direction.

"Clint!"

Dory squinted into the sunlight and saw a woman riding toward them, her pale blond hair streaming behind her in the breeze. Her face flushed, the blonde reined in the beautiful brown-and-white horse, stopping the animal only several feet from where they stood. She leaped down and rushed to throw her arms around Clint.

His arms instantly came up to lift her in the air. "Why, Sara Lynn, aren't you a sight for sore eyes," he said, grinning as he swept her in a circle before setting her back on the ground. "Every time I think you can't possibly get any prettier, you go and prove me dead wrong."

Laughing, she swatted his arm. "You always say that."

"Only because it's the God's honest truth."

The young woman groaned good-naturedly and smiled at Dory, curiosity sparkling in her blue eyes. "Hi, I'm Sara."

"Dory Richards," she said, extending her hand.

Sara accepted her offering, briefly wincing when Dory squeezed too hard.

Mentally kicking herself, Dory promptly released her. She tried not to look at Clint but caught the amused curve of his mouth out of the corner of her eye.

"When did you come home?" he asked Sara.

"Just yesterday. I couldn't miss the Fourth of July shindig, now could I?" She looped an arm through his, her cheeks tinted a becoming pink and gazed up at him with undisguised adoration.

Feeling like a fifth wheel, Dory turned back to loading the trailer. The younger woman couldn't be more than nineteen or twenty, but she clearly had a mile-wide crush on Clint. Probably just his type, too, a real girlie girl. Even after having been out riding, her make-up was perfect, her hair tousled to perfection by the breeze, and for heaven's sake, her jeans still had a crease in them.

"Hey, Dory. Relax a minute." Clint took the boards from her hands. "You're going to get overheated."

"I'll make lemonade," Sara offered. "Come on up to the house."

He touched a finger to the brim of his Stetson and nudged it upward, and then pulled a bandanna from his back pocket and mopped his forehead. "Thanks anyway, but we don't have time."

"Grover and Lenny are in the north pasture. I could go get them to help."

"Nah, we'll be done in a half hour or so." Clint's gaze narrowed on Dory. "You sore yet?"

She snorted. "I'm not the one who needed a break."

Grinning, he stuffed his bandanna back in his pocket. "Seriously, I don't want you to push too hard and end up out of commission all weekend."

"Oh, please." Dory adjusted her gloves.

"Hey, I have a vested interest in returning you alive. Kate will hurt me if I don't."

"Ah, I see. Nothing altruistic about your motives."

Sara's dramatic sigh netted her the attention she wanted. "I wish I could help but I don't think I'd be much use." She daintily put out her hands and wiggled her fingers. "Not with these nails." They were long, fake and pale pink, the tips sparkling with red, white and blue glitter.

Clint's patronizing smile appeared unnoticed by Sara. She merely beamed when he picked up one of her hands and brought the back to his lips for a quick kiss.

"These hands are a work of art. Wouldn't want to mess them up," he said, winking at her, before pulling on his gloves.

Sara giggled. "You better save me the first dance tomorrow night," she said, while backing toward her horse. "I mean it, Clint Manning. I call dibs and I have a witness."

"Wouldn't dream of dancing with anyone else first, Sara Lynn." He'd already started back to work.

"What dance?" Dory asked, stooping beside him to pick up a load of lumber. She hated dances. Didn't even know how to dance. In high school, proms had been her worst nightmare.

"What dance, she asks." Shaking his head in mock disapproval, he slid a stack of boards onto the pile, and then gave her a cocky wink. "Looks like you're in for an initiation this weekend."

3

THANKS TO DORY'S HARD WORK, they finished quicker than Clint had anticipated, and then headed back to the Sugarloaf. Still, making the unexpected pickup had put him behind schedule, what with the booths to build and the tables and chairs to set up for the barbecue tomorrow night. And since people tended to show up early in the morning, it looked as if he and the boys would be working until well after sundown. He really hated to put the crew out like that because it didn't seem right to work them so hard that they'd be too tuckered out to enjoy the festivities, but if they wanted to be ready in time, he didn't have much choice.

As if she'd read his mind, Dory asked, "What's next?"

"For you, I suggest a warm bath. Soak those muscles you used today." He looked over at her dirt-streaked face, cheeks flushed from exertion, and caught her eye-roll. Whether she wanted to admit it or not, she would be sore later. "You were a big help."

"What are *you* going to do?"

"Build the game booths."

"Today?"

"I guarantee you we'll have three dozen kids show up bright and early tomorrow morning, all of them raring to go."

"I knew the party started tomorrow but I assumed the

afternoon barbecue kicked it off. How many people are you expecting?"

"Generally between one-seventy and two hundred."

"Good grief."

He chuckled. "It's not so bad. They don't show up all at once. Except maybe for the rodeo and fireworks on Sunday, which is the last night."

"Is Kate in charge of providing all the food?"

"Yep, but don't worry, you saw how well she delegates." They both smiled at that, and then he added, "You okay with making another stop?"

"Sure. I don't know that we'll have room to pick up anything else, though." She twisted around to glance out the rear window at the overloaded trailer.

The way her T-shirt stretched over her breasts caught Clint's attention, and he drove right through a deep pothole. The truck bucked and pulled to the left. Reflexively, he threw out an arm to protect her from flying forward and came into contact with the soft round objects of his distraction. He quickly retreated but not before he momentarily lost control of the wheel.

"Look out."

A large dead tree partially blocked the road. He sharply turned the wheel but it was too late. The left front tire dipped into a rut and struck something hard and immobile. He managed to pull the truck back onto the road but skidded slightly, and he knew the rear tire had met the same fate as the front one. While applying the brakes, his gaze shot to the rearview mirror. The trailer had survived, although it had come a foot away from jackknifing.

His eyes met hers. "Are you okay?"

She nodded. "You?"

Grunting an affirmative, totally disgusted with himself, he threw the gearshift into Park.

"What happened?"

He jerked open the door, a string of curses springing to mind, but he bit them back as he climbed out.

"It feels like we lost the front tire," she said, and scrambled out after him.

He'd consider himself lucky if it were the only one. He suspected the rear tire had taken a hit, too. Crouching down, he surveyed the damage. The front tire was already flat, and he quickly spotted the gash in the rubber that had caused the trouble.

"Damn." Dory had come to stand beside him and stared at the ruined wheel. "I hate to tell you but the back tire is losing air, too. But it seems to be a slow leak so it could just be a small puncture."

Clint really had to work at holding on to his temper. None of this was her fault. The blame was totally his, and she didn't deserve the sarcasm simmering inside him. He pushed to his feet. "I hope you're right so we don't have to call the ranch for a tow. Everyone is busy enough."

"You have more than one spare?"

"Nope, but if it is a small puncture I have some of that spray stuff to use for a temporary fix."

"Give me the jack and I'll get started on the front tire while you check out the rear."

Clint barked out a laugh. "You're offering to change the tire?"

She blinked, clearly surprised at first, and then she narrowed her eyes. "And if I am?"

"You go sit in the shade and sip some water. I'll take care of this."

"Oh, brother."

"Are we gonna stand here arguing, or can we try to get back before the barbecue starts tomorrow?" He stalked to the back of the truck, suddenly and painfully aware that although the spare was accessible under the bed, the spray can was in his toolbox buried under a mountain of lumber.

"Don't get huffy with me. I wasn't the one driving like an idiot."

"Son of a—" He cut himself off, but vented his frustration by slamming an open hand on the side of the truck. Pain shot up his arm.

"What?"

He didn't say anything, just stared at the load of lumber. No way around it. He was going to have to move half the boards over to the other side to get to the toolbox. The hell of it was he knew better than to find himself in this predicament. Now he'd sucked Dory into the mess.

She didn't say another word. As if she sensed the problem, she got down on her haunches and worked at dislodging the spare stowed under the bed. Ashamed of himself, he hunkered down beside her, and took her by the shoulders.

Her upper arms were slim, but taut and lightly muscled under his grip, which didn't surprise him considering how hard she'd worked beside him. What did catch him off guard was his reluctance to release her, the sudden itch to run his palms down her arms and take her hands in his. Resisting the urge, he gently forced her aside and got to work. He figured he'd done enough harm for one day.

WHEN THEY RETURNED to the Sugarloaf Ranch, Dory offered to help unload the lumber even though she knew he'd turn her down. As soon as the words were out of her mouth she'd regretted them. There were two guys standing around, waiting to help, but no, she had to prove she was as good as any man, prove that she could keep up with Clint. God, when was she going to learn to back off and quit acting like a dope.

She stood off to the side, out of the way, grinding her teeth. She was fit and buff and as capable as most men when it came to physical labor. That was something to be proud of, not something to be kicking herself over. So what that she wasn't like Lisa or Kate or Jessica? Or most other women, for that matter. She was a tomboy, and always had been. That never bothered her, so why second-guess herself now?

Oh, heck, she knew why. She'd been a bully about changing the tire and hurt Clint's pride. Did she really have to prove she could change a tire faster than he could? No wonder he'd barely spoken to her the rest of the way back.

"You don't need to hang around," he said gruffly as the last of the lumber was unloaded and he walked past her. "Go grab a shower while there's still hot water."

She dabbed self-consciously at her smudged cheeks. "Are you going to start building the booths now?"

"That's the plan."

She half skipped to catch up to his longer strides as he headed toward the barn. "I'm pretty good with a hammer."

He slid her an exasperated glance. "I don't doubt it for a minute."

"Oh, come on, I'm sorry. I didn't mean to—" She cut herself short when she noticed that one of the men who'd helped unload was watching them with avid interest.

Clint whipped off his hat and smacked it against the front of his thigh. Without the brim shading his eyes, they looked incredibly green in the fading sunlight. "Kate might need some help in the kitchen. As far as the thing with the tire, you won fair and square. You beat me by a full three minutes." He bowed at the waist and extended his arm with a flourish. "My hat's off to you." His gaze staying level with hers, he added in a grouchy voice, "Did you catch all that, Curly?"

The short, paunchy, older man who'd been watching them quickly averted his eyes and hastened toward the corral where the other guy had gone back to working with a mustang.

"Look, I can't cook worth beans, okay? I won't be of any use to Kate."

Amusement hovered at the corners of his mouth. "Can you boil water?"

"With instructions, maybe."

"Hell, then maybe we ought to keep you out of the kitchen."

"Trust me. That would serve everyone well."

"Come on then," he said grudgingly. "I won't deny I could use the help."

She followed him into the massive barn that housed all sorts of tack, saddles and harnesses. Bales of hay were stacked in a maze, so high that she couldn't see where they were going. Hovering above the smell of leather and hay, the strong aroma of brewing coffee teased her nostrils. The air was warm and sticky, and hot coffee was the last thing that should appeal to her, but her mouth watered.

"The booths really aren't hard to put up," Clint said as he led her to a small shed tucked in the corner of the barn. "We don't care about them being too fancy. It's a simple frame with a canvas roof, enough for some shade."

"I'm surprised you don't keep everything ready to assemble each year."

"Normally we do, but the storage shed leaked last fall

and most of the boards and two-by-fours suffered too much water rot." He pulled on a string and a bare light-bulb flooded the small area with light. "Let's see, we need nails, hammers, a staple gun…"

Dory had stepped inside with him before she realized what little space was allowed by the floor-to-ceiling shelves and two large generators. She'd started backing out when he turned to her, his arm brushing her breast, his face so close to her face that his breath mingled with hers.

"Sorry," she murmured, bumping into the door frame behind her.

"My fault," he said, but didn't sound the least bit apologetic. His gaze lowered to her mouth. Automatically she moistened her lips. "If you've changed your mind and would rather take that shower, I won't hold it against you."

Was that a hint? She sniffed. Oh, God, she'd been sweating like a pig earlier.

"No, no, that's not what I meant." Laughing, he caught her wrist when she tried to flee. "We're in the same boat, honey. I'm not in a position to throw stones. Besides, you smell pretty good to me."

The teasing glint that had lit his eyes a second ago darkened, as his gaze once again rested on her lips. His hold on her wrist grew a fraction tighter, and she felt the pad of his thumb at her speeding pulse.

Dory held her breath and moved back a step.

Clint noisily cleared his throat. He dropped her wrist, and turned back to gathering supplies. "We've got seven booths to set up. Actually, eight if you count the ticket booth but if we're short on time we can set up a chair and beach umbrella for the seller. That's worked in the past. Curly and two other guys who've been mending fences are gonna help so we should finish before sundown."

She moved back farther so that she was standing just outside the doorway. The meager distance she'd put between them did little to slow down her racing heart. For one crazy second she'd actually thought again that he might kiss her. Which was ridiculous, of course. She'd merely been in his way. "You sell tickets?"

"About five years ago Kate had the idea of turning the games into a fund-raiser for the no-kill animal shelter in town. We've raised quite a bit of money since then," he said in a tone so normal it confirmed that she'd been insane about the potential kiss.

"What a great idea. Kate would come up with something like that. Want me to take some of those?"

He handed her three hammers and a level. "By the way, where are the other two who came with you?"

"No idea. I haven't seen them since we got here." Dory grinned. "But I wouldn't be looking to recruit them if I were you. I doubt either one knows which end of the hammer to use."

He chuckled. "Nah, I remember them. I didn't figure they would. Here. Can you manage this, too?"

She accepted the sack of nails he handed her, still feeling the sting of his remark. He'd remembered Lisa and Jessica but not her. The thing was, Dory had no business being surprised or upset. They were both gorgeous, and she'd always been just plain tomboy Dory.

4

AS LOATH AS SHE WAS to admit it, Dory was exhausted. She was sweaty and hungry and a gallon of water sounded good about now. The amount of physical labor she'd subjected herself to was taxing enough, but coupled with the eight-hour red-eye flight she'd taken to get here, and the short time since she'd returned from Cambodia, she knew she was close to her limit.

She stepped back from the structure she'd just completed, and set down her hammer before her arm fell off. Anyway, Clint really didn't need her anymore. Nearly a dozen men had returned from the pastures for their evening meal, but seeing that the project hadn't been completed, they'd all chipped in. Most of them weren't that handy with a hammer so the job still took longer than it should have, but finally, there was only one booth left to erect.

Picking up the bottle of water that Kate had brought her earlier, she took a long, cool sip and then scanned the field beyond the booths to the carousel that had been delivered an hour ago. The entire area had been designated the kids' zone, complete with giant waterslide, an inflated fun house with a trampoline-type bottom and a section cordoned off for pony rides. She saw Curly and Tom and Silas, whom she'd met earlier, but she couldn't find Clint.

"We're done. Chuck and Tom will finish the last booth." His voice came from behind her.

"Good." She started to turn but then stopped to stretch a kink out of her neck. "Gotta admit, I was ready to call it—"

He'd taken off his shirt. His smooth bronzed chest and broad shoulders gleamed with moisture, and for the life of her she couldn't remember what she was about to say. She tried to look away, but instead her gaze swept to the low ride of his jeans on his lean, narrow hips. His belly was flat and ridged with just enough muscle to make the view interesting.

She forced her attention upward before he noticed she was staring, and was relieved to find him using his shirt to wipe his face. She took another quick sip of water to relieve her parched throat.

He took a final swipe with his shirt, met her eyes and smiled. "Sorry, what did you say?"

"Ah, nothing." She shrugged. "Just that I was going to throw in the towel."

He nodded. "Kate reminded me that you'd flown all night. I apologize for using and abusing you."

She waved a dismissive hand. "Forget it. I was happy to help."

"Come on, I'll walk you back to the house. Supper should be ready soon."

She really wished he'd put his shirt on because she could hardly trust herself not to stare like a starstruck schoolgirl. Instead, she concentrated on the pinkish-orange clouds that streaked across the slate-blue sky, courtesy of the sun sitting low on the horizon behind them. "What time does it get dark?"

"In about half an hour. We cut it close, though we could've strung up some lights if we had to." They walked close together, their shoulders sometimes touching, and she tried to ignore the little shiver of pleasure the contact produced. "Tomorrow morning we'll set up the two tents and picnic tables," Clint continued. "Shouldn't take more than a couple of hours."

"I can help."

He snorted. "I think the boys and I can handle it. Only a few hands have regular chores assigned tomorrow. The rest will be free to help out with the party if they're needed."

"I should be of some use. It seems I'm much better with a hammer than most of you."

He stopped, and gave her a long, drawn-out look of astonishment. "You are really something else, you know that?"

"It's nothing to be shamed of. Just because you have a penis doesn't automatically make you a carpenter." She shrugged when his look of disbelief turned into a glare. "I'm sure you guys are probably great at rounding up cattle or whatever it is you normally do. I volunteered with Habitat for Humanity for two summers and learned how to use a hammer."

His jaw set, he again started toward the house, balling his shirt in a tight fist and squeezing. She had a feeling he'd have preferred it were her neck.

"Nothing personal," she said, hurrying to keep up with his accelerating pace. "But I am sorry if I hurt your feelings. Sometimes I forget how fragile the male ego is. Not just in humans. You'll find in every species that—"

He stopped abruptly and faced her. "Can't you for once act like a girl?"

She blinked, trying not to show how much his words had stung. It didn't matter that regret immediately flooded his features. Or that she was well aware of her lack of feminine appeal.

"I'm sorry. I didn't mean it." He passed a hand over his face, briefly covering his mouth. "I can't believe I said that."

She lifted a shoulder. "It's okay. Really. I get it."

"No, I was rude." He touched her arm. "You were great today, and you don't deserve me being a—"

"A pig," she finished sweetly.

He tugged down the brim of his hat so that she could no longer see his eyes. "Not what I was gonna say, but yeah…I guess that's appropriate."

Damn right. "Forget it. Like you said, dinner is probably waiting." She didn't care. Not really, she thought as she continued toward the house. It was a beautiful evening. She was thrilled to be able to spend some time with the gang after not seeing them for so long. They'd have a nice dinner, and then gab until they couldn't keep their eyes open any longer. Just like the old days. This was their weekend. She refused to give Clint another thought.

BY THE TIME IT WAS Dory's turn to use the bathroom she shared with Jessica, the small room was hot and steamy, and for a second she felt as if she were back in Cambodia. Except in the jungle there was no hot shower, no privacy and no worrying about how you looked when you finally sat down to fill your belly.

She liked her job, and the guys she worked with were all top-notch in their field, as well as being a good bunch to hang out with. But she wondered if the prolonged isolation she endured wasn't skewing her view of social correctness.

After shampooing and rinsing her hair, she wanted nothing more than to linger under the soothing warm water, but that would make her late for dinner. So she dried off, wrapped herself in the luxuriously plush pink towel, and stood in front of the fogged mirror. Perfect. She didn't want to have to look at her reflection, anyway.

Annoyed with her attitude, she grabbed the comb from her carry-on and dragged the teeth through her wet hair. Normally she'd let it air-dry but she knew darn well Jessica and Lisa would be getting gussied up tonight. Normally that wouldn't matter to Dory, but she didn't want to seem uncouth, either. After all, they were adults, not indifferent college kids anymore, she thought as her gaze rested on the makeup Jessica had left in her corner of the white-tiled countertop.

Dory had tried eyeliner and eye shadow once. The experience had been a total disaster. She generally stuck to mascara, and only when she remembered that she had a tube in her backpack. Luckily, with the amount of sun exposure she received from working outside, she never worried about foundation or blush.

Still staring at the intimidating assortment of cosmetics, she nibbled her lower lip. It wouldn't hurt to take another stab at it. Jessica wouldn't care if she used any of this stuff, in fact, she'd probably be elated. She'd always tried to get Dory to make more of her appearance.

Can't you for once act like a girl?

His words reverberated in her head like the grating sound of a bird's screech bouncing off canyon walls.

Why was she letting his thoughtless remark get to her? If anything, she shouldn't have let him off so easily. She should've made him define *girl* and watch him squirm. So what if Dory wasn't a Sara Lynn. She wouldn't apologize for that. For the past two years she'd worked exclusively with men, the only woman for hundreds of miles and still hadn't sparked an interest in any of them. She never questioned it. Never gave it a thought. Until now.

Was she really that hopeless?

Furiously, she wiped the mirror until there was a small area clear enough to see her reflection, and then started grabbing the various compacts of eye shadow, liner sticks and lip pencils. This was going to be tricky, drying her hair and deftly applying the unfamiliar makeup in a short period of time. Briefly she thought about calling for Jessica who Dory could hear moving about in the adjoining room, but she wasn't up to the inevitable bombardment of questions. Until this morning, they hadn't seen her for five years. Maybe if she showed up wearing makeup, they'd believe she'd changed.

She went to work, first drying her hair, though leaving it damp, and then tackling the face paint. She felt clumsy but worked quickly and within minutes, blinked at the garish face that stared back. Her confidence crumpled. The black around her eyes made her look like a raccoon, and the gray shadow resembled one of those goth chicks that hung around the mall. The pale pink lipstick was okay, but that was it. Pretty sad.

So much for *acting like a girl.* Disappointed yet annoyed with her foolishness, she plucked two tissues from the box and started to wipe her face, careful not to end up with black streaks on her cheeks. By the time she was done, something miraculous had happened. The residual makeup that remained was perfect. The smudged smoky color around her brown eyes made them look bigger and more exotic. The difference was subtle yet totally amazing.

She nervously licked her lips, totally screwing up the

lipstick, and had to reapply it after slipping on a clean pair of jeans and one of the denim blouses she'd brought. After a final check in the mirror, she left her room and headed toward the sound of Kate's and Lisa's laughter. They were coming from the kitchen, carrying platters of sliced chicken and beef and veggie trays.

"Just in time," Kate said, catching sight of her and motioning with a tilt of her head for Dory to follow. "Because the kitchen has been tied up all day, we're just having sandwiches. And then sinfully rich chocolate cake."

"Sounds good to me. I'm so hungry I'd even eat eggplant at this point."

Making a sound of disgust, Jessica came from behind with a pitcher of water and a bottle of red wine. "That's pretty desperate."

"What can I do?" Dory asked.

"I heard you've been busting your fanny all day." Lisa slid her tray onto the oak dining room table and then looked up, her blue eyes widening. "Whoa, welcome to the age of glamour."

"What?" She hadn't meant to sound peevish. Oh, God, when the other two turned to stare at her she wanted to crawl under the table.

Kate's slaw-jawed surprise didn't help. "You look terrific. When did you start wearing makeup?"

She shrugged. "A couple of years ago." At the ridiculous lie, heat crawled up her neck, and she turned, pretending to be looking for something. "Should I get silverware?"

Jessica got in her face and grinned. "I'm so proud. Our little girl is all grown up."

"Very funny. Now knock it off." So much for subtle. She glanced toward the stairs that led to the bedrooms.

If Clint showed up now and heard all the teasing, she'd just die of embarrassment.

Although she couldn't seem to hide her amusement, Kate gave the other two a warning look and then dug into the drawer of an oak china hutch that matched the table. Producing a stack of beige linen napkins, she handed them to Dory along with a handful of forks and knives. "You can set these out."

Lisa passed out dinner and dessert plates, while Jessica went to get water glasses.

Kate laid serving forks beside the platters of meat and sliced tomatoes, and then remembering that they needed mayo and mustard, returned to the kitchen.

After completing her task, Dory glanced at the grandfather clock near the stairs. Where was Clint, anyway? Or Kate's other brother, for that matter.

"Let's get the wine poured," Lisa said, and popped the cork. "Pass me some glasses, will you?"

The other two returned, and they all took their seats. Kate started passing the food, and Dory realized only four places had been set. Good thing she hadn't gotten all made up for Clint. Clearly he'd decided to bail on dinner.

5

THE NEXT DAY STARTED OUT hot even before the sun inched up over the mesquite trees dotting the eastern slopes. Clint squinted at the haze of dust kicked up by his brother's horse as he galloped south, intent on riding the fence line. Joe had always liked to stick to daily operations rather than get involved with the weekend's festivities, but today he'd been particularly stubborn about putting distance between himself and the fray. Even after Clint had practically begged him to swap places with him.

He knew that facing Dory was inevitable, and that it wasn't going to be easy. Shame had shadowed him the whole night, and he'd deserved every last minute of feeling as if a noose were tightening around his neck. Not that he thought she'd gone running to tell Kate what a jerk her brother was. He was pretty sure Dory was more the type to pretend the incident had never happened. Except he'd seen the hurt look on her face.

Figuring his presence at supper wouldn't be welcome, he'd eaten with the men in the bunkhouse, and then drank beer and played Texas Hold 'Em until midnight. But because his mind hadn't been on poker, he'd lost a couple hundred bucks. If that wasn't bad enough, most of it had been to their foreman, whose irritating cackle and penchant for pointing out every dumb play Clint made had just about pushed him over the edge.

He downed his third cup of black coffee, relieved that the dull ache in his head from too much beer and too little sense was finally easing up. So far, only one of the tents had been erected and it was already close to eight-thirty. Last night's jump start on the weekend's festivities had put them behind schedule. Most of the men helping with the party preparations were slow moving, probably hung over, and he couldn't say a word because he was such a damn poor example.

"Good morning," Dory said cheerfully as she came from behind and stood beside him, her hands wrapped around an oversize blue mug.

He eyed her warily, but she didn't give any indication that she was still upset. "Mornin.' Sleep well?"

"Boy, did I ever." She wore jeans, no holes this time, and a snug white T-shirt tucked into her waistband, revealing a narrow waist and curvy hips. "Though we stayed up too late talking."

"I was up late, too," he grumbled. "Losing money."

"Poker?"

"Yep." Was it really gonna be this easy? As if he hadn't opened his big mouth and stuck his size-eleven boot into it. Had she already forgiven him?

She smiled. "Been there, done that. After work, and having read every book you can carry in with you, there's not much to do in the jungle for months at a time." She took a sip of coffee and then frowned at him over the rim of the mug. "Why are you looking at me like that?"

"Me?" He'd been staring at the tiny dimple that appeared near the corner of her mouth. Something else he hadn't noticed yesterday. "Nothing. We've got some coffee brewing in the barn. Want a refill?"

"Sure. If you want, I can get some for both of us."

"Yeah, thanks." He handed her his mug. "Just black," he called as she started to walk away, noting a slight natural sway to her hips. Interesting how different she looked with her shirt tucked in.

"What time you expect the kids to start showin' up?" Pete's gravelly voice startled Clint out of his preoccupation with the way Dory's jeans hugged her backside.

"I'd say about an hour and a half. We have to get the other tent up before then." Clint pulled his hat brim down in deference to the sun. "I want the tools and equipment stored before those kids start running wild around here."

"We could rope off the area if you think—"

A howl came from inside the barn. And then a scream. Clint and Pete exchanged glances, and then they both took off at a run. Clint quickly outdistanced the older man and entered the barn first. Newly stacked bales of hay blocked his way and obscured his view. He darted through the maze toward the kitchenette in back where they kept the coffee.

"Dory!"

"It's okay. I'm all right."

Following the sound of her voice, he found her near the coffeepot, standing with her back to him. "What happened?"

Without turning around, she brushed off the front of her jeans. "Whoever said everything is bigger in Texas wasn't kidding. You have cats the size of Canada."

Clint grinned. "That would be Sylvester."

"What's wrong?" Huffing and puffing, Pete shuffled in. He bent over to catch his breath, his gaze bouncing between Clint and Dory.

"Sylvester," was all Clint had to say.

"Damn cat." Pete snorted. "If he weren't such a good mouser I'd have cut him loose up in the hills long ago."

That was a lie. Pete wouldn't admit it for all the chewing tobacco in Houston, but he loved that monstrous gray tabby. "Sorry about that. Sylvester can be territorial," Clint said, wondering why she wouldn't turn around. "I didn't think to warn you." He moved closer. "Are you sure you're okay?"

"Yes." She threw a nervous glance over her shoulder at him. "I can't believe I screamed." She sighed. "Like a girl."

Clint might have appreciated the joke more if he didn't suspect something was wrong. He moved around to face her and saw their mugs lying at her feet. And then he noticed she was favoring her arm. The skin inside of her wrist had reddened where the hot coffee obviously burned her.

"Ah, Dory. We'll put some ointment on it."

"It's nothing, really. I've had much worse."

"What did that damn critter do now? Hope he didn't scratch you." Pete came to look, taking off his hat and peering at Dory.

She hunched her shoulders. "Please, it's okay. I'm going to return to the house to rinse it off and change. Go back to what you were doing."

Clint sensed her tension, noted the self-conscious posture. "Go on, Pete, I'll take care of her."

"I feel awful responsible, that being my cat and all." Despite his words, Pete seemed as if he wanted to bolt.

"Pete, that tent has to go up now."

"You got it, boss." He jammed his hat back on his wiry gray hair as he backed away. "Sorry about that, miss."

"Not a problem," she said, and waited until Pete disappeared before lowering the arm she'd been cradling.

"We've got a first aid—" Clint lost this train of thought when he saw the front of her T-shirt.

Splashed with black coffee, the white cotton clung to her like a second skin. Her hardened nipples poked at the wet fabric. It looked as if she weren't wearing a bra. But then he saw the faint pink outline. His body responded, and then shame set in. Guiltily, he snapped out of his inappropriate musings.

"How's your chest?" he asked.

Her eyebrows shot up.

"You know what I mean," he muttered, and went in search of the first-aid kit, which he found tucked in a lower cabinet.

When he came back around, Dory had pulled up her shirt and was inspecting her smooth flat belly. Nothing indecent about the amount of skin she exposed. But the view was more than he could handle. He handed her the kit, and got the hell out.

AN HOUR LATER, she'd changed her ruined shirt, ministered to the burn on her wrist, and still Lisa and Jessica weren't dressed. Assured she wasn't needed in the kitchen, Dory walked out the back door and saw that both tents were now up, canopying four long picnic-style tables, benches and chairs. Coming from the front of the house, she heard the shrieks of excited kids.

She shaded her eyes against the brilliant sun and noticed Clint gesturing wildly to a pair of cowhands, who immediately trotted toward the carousel. She guessed they hadn't anticipated the early arrival of the children. Torn between staying out of the way and offering to help, the decision was made when Clint gestured for her to join him.

"Feel like selling tickets or manning one of the game booths?" he asked.

"Tell me what you want me to do."

"Come with me."

She half jogged to keep up as his longer legs ate up the ground to the wooden folding chair and umbrella that was set up in front of the booths. On the chair sat a metal money box and a huge roll of generic yellow tickets.

"There's change in the box and each ticket costs a quarter. The rides and games all require tickets. But everybody knows the drill, and frankly, no one will turn a kid away if they don't have a ticket. Any questions?" He sounded business-like, yet when she shook her head, he gently touched her arm. "Let's see," he said, turning over her wrist so he could inspect the injured skin.

"See? It's nothing." Her pulse quickened when the pad of his thumb gently stroked her arm.

"Not bad." He met her eyes and something unidentifiable and kind of scary passed between them.

She cleared her throat and pulled away.

"The chili cook-off starts shortly after noon," he said, stuffing his hands in his back pockets. "I'm gonna go check on the stoves in the contestants' booths. I'll be back to make sure someone relieves you."

"Don't worry about me." She picked up the metal box, sat down and set it on her lap, feeling somewhat shaky. Clint's dark green eyes and gentle touches were tipping her off balance. It was crazy, and she didn't know how to react to him. "Go."

He started to leave, and then turned back to her. "You're a good sport, Dory. Thanks."

"Sure." She shrugged, feeling a bit low suddenly.

Pretending to acquaint herself with the money box and tickets, she kept her head bowed until he was gone.

Dory, the good sport. Dory, one of the guys. Dory, the dependable. None of those tags had ever bothered her before, and she hated that they did now. It wasn't as if a man like Clint would ever be interested in her as a woman, but for just a few minutes, she'd felt a connection with him. Weird, because she was never foolish like this about men. She not only understood her feminine limitations, but in general, she truly lacked interest. What was it about Clint's indifference that depressed her?

She blew out a frustrated breath and then was relieved to be distracted by her first customer, a cute little freckled girl of about seven. After making the child's change and passing over her tickets, Dory's gaze automatically scanned the growing crowd in search of Clint. He was clear across the field, but she spotted him right away because he was taller than most of the other men.

He was talking and laughing with someone, and Dory strained so hard to see who it was, she nearly fell off her chair. But she caught a glimpse of the tall, leggy blonde around whose shoulders he'd casually slipped an arm.

Checking on the chili cook-off booths. Right. She adjusted the metal box on her lap, and muttered when she accidentally ripped off a fingernail.

"Excuse me, miss." It was the ranch foreman, whom she'd met yesterday.

"Hi, Silas. Need some tickets?"

"No, ma'am. Seems we're in a pickle and Pete thinks I should talk to you."

"Yes?"

"We need help in one of the booths."

She lifted a shoulder. "Sure, but what about selling tickets?"

"I can do that for the time being," he said, abruptly removing his hat and grinning. "But we need a pretty gal like yourself for the booth. The kissing booth."

6

BY THE TIME CLINT had made sure the stage was ready for the first band that was scheduled to begin playing at noon, the rides were running and the dunking booth operational, he was itching for another shower and a cold drink. Barring any unforeseen problems with the lighting for tonight or the half barrels they'd set up for the barbecue, his job was done and he could enjoy the festivities. He did have one thing left to do…find a replacement for Dory. He'd left her sitting under that umbrella longer than he'd intended, and felt badly about the inconvenience, but he planned to make it up to her.

He headed toward the house and the makeshift ticket booth set up close to the driveway. But as he got closer he saw a teenage girl with a mass of curly red hair now selling tickets. He was glad someone had relieved Dory, but where was she? He spun around, scanning the crowd, starting with the group of people gathered around the lemonade stand. There were still more kids than adults milling about. All that would change in the next hour, but for now she should have been easy to spot.

Several cowhands had lined up at one of the booths, but she wasn't among them. When Clint shaded his eyes, he saw that she was behind the counter, collecting tickets. Who the hell put her there? Kate was gonna kick his ass if she thought he'd made her friend work the entire weekend. Sighing, he strode toward Dory. But stopped dead in his tracks when young Sam Taylor leaned over the counter and laid a big sloppy kiss on Dory that sent the whole line of men to hooting and hollering.

Dory threw her head back and laughed. "That counted as two, cowboy," she said, holding out her palm. "Hand over four more tickets."

Grinning, Sam dug into his pocket and slapped a handful of yellow tickets into her hand. "That's enough for two more," he said, nudging his hat back and leaning toward her.

"You had your turn, you ornery young buck, now git to the back of the line if you want seconds." Curly's protest was joined by several of the other men, apparently from neighboring ranches because Clint didn't recognize them.

Of course he hadn't paid much attention to the men. He was still too stunned over the fact that Dory was manning the kissing booth. He took off his hat, and used the back of his sleeve to wipe his eyes. Dory looked different. For one thing, she wasn't wearing a T-shirt but a denim blouse with the top two buttons left undone, showing a little skin and hint of cleavage. Nothing too revealing, just enough to whet a man's appetite. Her hair was down, too, a bit wild and wavy around her face, and he was pretty sure she was wearing makeup.

"Hey, boss, ain't you getting in line?" Pete stood off to the side, hat in hand, his gray hair damp, the usual frizz neatly slicked back. "Go on," he said. "You can go ahead of me."

Clint stared at the older man, who was real funny about admitting to his age, but Clint knew he was in his mid-sixties. Yet here he was, suddenly blushing like a young girl going to her first dance. "You've got to be kidding."

"It's for a good cause, ain't it?" Pete muttered gruffly.

"Where's Melanie Cooper? Isn't she supposed to be taking the first shift?"

"Called and said she'd be about an hour late so we asked Dory if she wouldn't mind doin' the honors. Didn't make no sense the booth bein' idle."

Clint's gaze went back to Dory. This was crazy. The kissing booth had always been popular and traditionally tied with target shooting for earning the most money, but he'd never seen this kind of participation from guys like Pete or old Gus, who was second in line.

"I'm warning you, no tongue," Dory said with a wagging finger at Curly as he stepped up for his turn. Color filled his chubby cheeks. Even his ears turned red.

The men all laughed raucously at her teasing. Flustered, Curly handed her his tickets and gave her a quick peck on the cheek.

"I was just kidding you, Curly," she assured him, and before he could move away, took his face in her hands and gave him a sweet kiss on the mouth.

Grinning, Curly stumbled backward, and then nearly ran Clint down as he got back in line.

Still baffled, Clint moved to the side so he wasn't blocking the growing stream of customers. It wasn't that Dory wasn't cute enough to garner this kind of attention, in fact, he thought she looked better each time he saw her. But every year they'd unabashedly roped the prettiest, sexiest girls in the county to tempt the men to part with their money for the animal shelter. That's why the booth always did so well.

Dory clearly had her own brand of charm. The way she

teased the men, especially the old-timers, put them at ease, and damned if nearly every single one of them didn't return to the back of the line for a second or third kiss.

When it was Pete's turn, he surprised everyone by grabbing Dory and tipping her backward for a long, loud smooch. She came up sighing dramatically and fanning herself, prompting peals of laughter from the rest of the men.

"Hey, boss, you'd better get in line before we tucker this little gal out," one of the boys yelled to Clint.

Dory apparently overheard and snapped a look in his direction. Judging by her startled expression, she hadn't known he'd been watching, and she suddenly seemed self-conscious. But then she tossed her hair back, and lifted her chin in challenge. "Step on up, cowboy. I promise not to bite," she said, and winked exaggeratedly at the men, who were lapping up her antics like thirsty dogs at the trough.

"Looks as if you're doing just fine without my business," he said, caught off guard by the realization that he wanted to kiss her. Not a token peck in front of the crowd, but one of those slow wet kisses that made his blood simmer. The knowledge shook him. When had he started thinking of Dory in those terms?

"Chicken," she taunted, her glittering eyes locked with his as she plucked the tickets from the hand of her next customer.

Clint smiled. Oh, he planned on kissing her, all right. Later. Without an audience. In fact, if she were willing, and he was pretty sure she would be, he planned on doing a whole lot more than kissing.

TWO HOURS, a glass of lemonade and half a gallon of water later, Dory's mouth was still drier than the

Mohave Desert. So far she'd serviced over a hundred customers, most of them repeats, but she was miffed that Clint had long disappeared. More than miffed, she was disappointed. Which she knew was ridiculous. He probably had a date for the weekend. Maybe that blonde she saw him with earlier.

She needed a break. Better yet, she needed someone else to take over the booth. She was tired and she'd run out of clever lines to keep the men entertained. She knew Kate had sent Jessica on an errand regarding the chili cook-off, so she wasn't available. Lisa had eagerly gone off in search of the older brother, Joe. Dory supposed she could ask Pete to furnish a replacement. Although it wasn't as if she had anything better to do, and with the line never seeming to end she'd raised a lot of money for the no-kill shelter.

Scanning the crowd, she still saw no sign of Clint, however, she did see Brad, a good-looking but cocky ranch hand from the Double R, getting in back of the line. He'd come through twice already, the second time behaving more boldly than she'd liked. She'd made a joke, and given him a gentle shove. But if he pulled anything funny again, she'd make him think twice about being a jackass.

While keeping an eye out for Pete, she dispensed with six more customers. And then it was Brad's turn again. She braced herself, wishing she'd thought to put up a Keep Your Hands to Yourself sign.

She smiled sweetly at him as he stepped up with his fist full of tickets. "You, I should charge double," she said.

"What?" He flashed her a broad smile. He had great teeth, she'd give him that, but he smelled like beer. "And here I thought you might be giving me a couple of freebies."

"Right. That'll happen," she murmured, and stuffed the tickets into the assigned box. "Now, you mind your manners, young man, or—"

"Or what?" Grinning, Brad slid an arm around her waist and pulled her against him. Regarding him in wide-eyed shock, she was about to protest, when he pressed a wet sloppy kiss to her lips. It was in the next second that she saw Clint, standing several feet away, next to a petite big-breasted redhead wearing a low-cut blouse and tight jeans.

He moved lightning fast, his expression dark and threatening, as he cupped a hand on Brad's shoulder. "What the hell are you doing?"

Brad blinked at him. "I paid for the kiss."

"That's not the kind of kiss the lady is offering," Clint said quietly, his fingers subtly tightening on the other man's shoulder.

If it hadn't been for Brad's beer breath, Dory might've told Clint to buzz off and go worry about his top-heavy date. Instead, she pried Brad's hands from her waist. "That's going to cost you, buster."

"I'll be back." He winked and then strutted toward the refreshment booth.

"Sorry about that," Clint said, irritation lingering in his stormy green eyes. "We've never had a problem before. The guys are usually respectful."

"It wasn't a big deal. You didn't have to step in. I could've easily handled him."

"That's right. You can handle everything."

She glared at him. "Your date is waiting."

"My what?" He frowned, and then followed her pointed look past him. "Wendy's not my date." He motioned for the redhead, who promptly sidled up to him. "She's your replacement."

"Oh." Dory smiled ruefully. "Hi."

"Hey." Wendy gave her a perky grin and then waved to the lineup. "Hi ya, boys. How're all y'all doing this afternoon?"

They responded with a chorus of enthusiastic greetings.

Laughing, Wendy stepped into the booth and made a shooing motion. "Now, you go have some fun with Clint. Sweet-talk him into winning you one of those adorable stuffed teddy bears. He won't brag, but he's the best shot in the county."

Dory didn't have to be told twice to leave. She gladly slipped out of the booth, the grunts of disappointment coming from the men in line doing wonders for her ego. Their reaction was all in good fun, though, and didn't seem to faze Wendy, who immediately got to work.

"Does she do this every year?" Dory asked as Clint steered her toward the lemonade stand.

"Yep, for the last nine or ten."

"She doesn't even look that old."

"Bet she'd love to hear that. She's been married for at least eight years and just had her third child two months ago."

"No way."

"I wouldn't lie to you, honey." One side of his mouth hiked up, and he pressed a hand to the small of her back to guide her left when she'd started to veer right.

An innocent touch for certain, but heat shot up her spine and pooled inside her belly. "You know, you don't have to babysit me."

"Yes, I do. I owe you."

Disappointment replaced the warmth. "No, you don't. I was happy to participate."

"Not for pulling a shift. The shelter owes you for that, and I'm sure they're very appreciative." A mischievous glint lit his eyes. "No, ma'am. I owe you for calling me chicken."

She started to laugh, and then realized they weren't headed for the lemonade stand. They were going toward the dunking booth.

7

AT THE LOOK ON HER FACE, Clint smiled to himself. He knew exactly what she was thinking because he'd planted the seed. He stopped directly in front of the dunking booth and watched as a boy of about twelve, carefully aimed for the target, hit it dead-on and dropped the local football coach into the trough of water. The boys awaiting their turns all cheered.

"I'm not doing that," she stated flatly. "I'm not that good a sport."

Chuckling, he casually draped an arm around her shoulders. She tensed and moistened her lips. His attention drew to her mouth, to the damp sheen that made her lips glisten a pale pink. And then the most shocking thing happened. Irrational jealousy slithered through him. How many men had kissed those lips today? Seventy? A hundred?

He gave himself a mental shake and lowered his arm. "What would you like to do? The chili cook-off samples aren't ready yet, and the ribs and chicken are still in the smoker for tonight, but there are hot dogs and burgers on the grill."

"I could definitely eat."

Good. Clint knew she wouldn't be shy about eating. "Let's go get something and listen to the band for a while."

"Don't you have stuff to do?"

"Only if an emergency arises. You like margaritas?"

She seemed hesitant. "Look, I can entertain myself."

"You didn't answer my question."

She gave him a bland look. "Frozen ones?"

"Probably not out here, but I have kitchen privileges."

She started to protest about not wanting special treatment, and what the hell, he slid his arm around her again and drew her alongside him. That promptly shut her up. But she walked so stiffly he didn't know if he should laugh or be insulted.

At the food tent, they got a burger and a hot dog each, a bag of chips to share, and then decided on cold beer instead of margaritas. They found a free table, and then ate and talked for over an hour. She had dozens of questions about what he did on the ranch and about the changes he wanted to make. At first he'd put her off. No point in talking about what couldn't be, since Joe was as likely to change his mind about modernizing as a dog could change his bark.

But with her intelligent brown eyes and genuine interest, Dory had him jabbering like a magpie about everything from using digital technology to shoe horses to the use of helicopters for roundup. Ironically it was the slew of well-intentioned interruptions that finally got to him. Just neighbors being neighborly, but he wanted Dory to himself.

As soon as the last chip was eaten, he cleared their remains, and asked, "Do you know how to ride?"

"I take it you mean a horse."

He pulled her to her feet. "Honey, this *is* a ranch."

"My parents gave me riding lessons for my sixteenth birthday, but it's been a while since I've saddled up."

"Your hippie parents? How very middle-class of them."

"They accidentally made a killing in real estate when

I was eleven." She smiled wryly. "But they're still hippies at heart. Where are we going?"

"I want to show you more of the ranch."

"What if someone needs you here?"

"For as many years as we've been putting on this shindig, if there's a problem they can sure figure it out." He showed her a shortcut to the stables, briefly pulling Pete aside to let him know he'd be gone for a while.

One of the newer cowhands had a question about a recent delivery of new tack, which Clint fielded while preparing his mount. He kept an eye on Dory while she saddled the gentle bay mare he'd chosen for her, and quickly found that she knew exactly what she was doing. No surprise. The woman took first prize for versatility.

They rode off without further interruption under a sky that had clouded just enough to buffer the unrelenting afternoon sun. The land was dry, and Clint would have preferred to show her the place in early spring when the pastures were emerald-green and wildflowers covered the gently rolling slopes. But even now there was a certain stark beauty he'd always appreciated and he had a feeling Dory could, too.

For the next half hour, they mostly rode in silence. He had a special place in mind where he wanted to take her. When he rode the east fence line, he frequented that particular spot to water his horse or jump in for a cooling dip himself. Even in the heat of July, the area was still lush and magically green thanks to an underground spring.

He'd taken other women there, twice, when he was younger, and now he had the foolish wish that he hadn't, that this could be an oasis he'd shared only with Dory. Man, the heat really had to be getting to him. He slowed them down, anxious to see her face when they rounded the bend.

"Does your family own all of this?" Dory asked, shading her eyes and twisting around in her saddle.

"As far as you can see."

"You can't possibly work this much land. You'd need hundreds of men."

"Yep." He wished she hadn't brought up the subject.

"That's why you want to use helicopters."

"Partly. We're almost there."

"Where?"

"Hold on." He reined in Lobo so that he stayed abreast of her, and watched her face as the spring came into view.

She didn't disappoint him. Her eyes widened and a flush of excitement stole across her cheeks. "Oh, my God."

"Beautiful, isn't it?"

"I'm—I'm speechless."

Clint grinned. "That won't last long."

"I'll let that remark slide," she said, her gaze transfixed on the small haven. Flicking her reins, she galloped ahead of him, then stopped at the water's edge and swung out of her saddle.

He caught up, dismounted and stood beside her.

"This is heaven," she whispered.

"It is." He wasn't looking at the miniature falls rippling over mossy rocks or the cascading pink wildflowers. He couldn't stop staring at Dory.

THE CHIRPING OF BIRDS and the sound of moving water rose above the silence. Nothing seemed real. The grass was almost too green, the water so clear Dory could see the rocks lining the bottom. They were smooth and glassy and looked more like gemstones.

The actual pool was really small, like something out of a fairy tale.

"Well?" He gently brushed the hair off her cheek.

She slowly turned to meet his eyes. "Well," she repeated awkwardly, her pulse quickening. "The horses could probably use a drink."

His gaze lowered to her mouth, and he took the reins from her hands. "Hope you saved one of those kisses for me."

"That'll be four tickets."

His mouth curved in a lazy smile. He looked so calm and cool, while her voice had come out coarse and her palms were clammy. She rubbed them down the front of her jeans.

"I'll be sure to pay you when we get back." He wrapped both their reins around a tree branch. "I assume you'll let me run a tab."

Her heart beat triple time. "On second thought, I've retired from that gig."

"Glad to hear that." He captured one of her hands and tugged her toward him. "Because this is strictly personal."

She hesitated a moment, her thoughts a maddening jumble of confusion and disbelief. "Did you bring me out here to take advantage of me?"

"Yep."

She laughed, the sound shaky as he slid his arms around her. She looped hers around his neck, enjoying the warm solid feel of her breasts pressed against his strong chest. He kissed the tip of her nose and then her chin, before claiming her mouth. His touch was gentle at first, more a light nibble, a coaxing brush of her lips with his. But then as if he could hold back no longer, he tightened his arms around her waist and ran the tip of his tongue across her lower lip, then along the seam, until she opened for him.

He'd hardened immediately, his arousal thrusting insistently against her belly as he deepened the kiss, his tongue boldly touching the fleshy inside of her cheek, the roof of her mouth, the back of her teeth. She pushed her fingers through his thick dark hair, and he ran his hands down her back and over her backside, cupping her there and pulling her harder against him. A tremor shook her off balance. For a second she thought the ground had moved, and then realized it was her own body quaking inside.

Unable to catch her breath, she pulled away. He regarded her blearily, the desire in his eyes so intense it made her belly clench. "Someone will see us," she whispered.

"There's nobody out here." He stroked the back of his hand down her cheek, lightly grazed her jaw and then toyed with the top button of her blouse.

"If someone did ride up, we wouldn't see them until it was too late." Her nipples tightened and strained against her restrictive bra. She wanted him to shoot down her objections, to show her that he wanted her as much as she wanted him.

"We'd hear them."

"But—"

He touched a finger to her lips. "Everyone is at the barbecue. The only reason we should stop is if you want to."

"I don't."

He smiled, and slid the first button free.

Had any woman ever said no to Clint Manning? Dory seriously doubted it. But she didn't care. There wasn't even the teeniest part of her that didn't want him.

She wasn't concerned that she probably wasn't as experienced as the women he normally slept with. Sadly,
she did wish she'd worn a better bra.

He undid the next button, and then the next, before
pulling the hem of her shirt from her jeans. The remaining buttons he unfastened much quicker and before she
knew it, her blouse was totally off, leaving her in the
ugly white bra. He didn't seem to notice, but reached
around to unhook it, while feathering kisses along the
side of her neck. After sliding the straps down her arms,
he kissed each bare shoulder.

The sun heated her bare skin, the longing in his face
seared the rest of her. He dropped the bra onto the grass
and gazed with appreciation at her exposed breasts.
Her nipples were as hard as saltwater pearls.

"Stay right where you are," he said, as he backed up.
"I got carried away and I'm doing this backward."

She stiffened, feeling horribly vulnerable suddenly
as she watched him dig into his saddlebag. He pulled
out a blanket and shook it out over the tall grass.

She blinked. "You had this planned."

"Let's say I was really hopeful." His mouth curved
in a sexy grin that he'd probably perfected at puberty.
"Come here."

She did as he asked, amazed that she could move so
gracefully. With the hungry way he looked at her it was
hard to still feel self-conscious. Powerful and desirable,
yes. Even sexy. She'd never experienced anything like
this before, as if she were truly alive after being
dormant for so long.

He lowered himself to the blanket first, smoothing
his palm over the surface before urging her to sit beside
him.

She shook her head. "Take your clothes off first."

It took him only seconds to lose his shirt and pull off his boots. When he unsnapped his jeans, she wisely got down on her knees while she had the poise to do it. The bulge straining his fly had her jumpy and near bursting with anticipation.

Without thinking, she unzipped her own jeans and pushed them down her hips while she watched him mirror her movements. A beat ahead of her, he pulled off his boxers. At the sight of his thick hardened cock, her throat constricted. With the grace of a hippo, she fell onto her fanny and kicked her way out of her jeans.

Clint helped her, his gaze touching her intimately. "Wow," he said, with a ghost of a smile. "You really are a girl."

8

SHE SMACKED HIS ARM. "You're hilarious."

"Couldn't resist," he murmured, the teasing suddenly gone from his face as he studied her breasts. His nostrils flared slightly, and then he lowered his mouth to her nipple.

He used his tongue and teeth to seduce a yearning that she'd never known. Heat raged through her body, and though she wanted to touch him, too, she closed her eyes, helpless to do anything but lie back and revel in the delicious sensations rippling through her.

He slid the hand on her hip down to her thigh, and then molded his palm to her butt with a light squeeze. She arched toward him and reached for his swollen cock, smooth and rock hard, the crown as slick as the wetness between her thighs. At her touch, a low primal sound came from his throat, emboldening her, and she started to pump him.

"Ah, Dory." He lifted his head, his eyes glazed with desire, before they drifted closed. "In my pocket…I have a condom," he said, sliding a hand up her inner thigh.

She sucked in a breath when he unerringly made contact with her clit. He slowly circled one finger over the sensitized nub, though how he managed with her thighs clamped tightly together she didn't know. It had been so long since she'd been touched this intimately that her instinct was to defend and flee. She forced herself to relax, to accept the pleasure he offered.

When the first spasm hit, she was so shocked she released his shaft and clutched his arm. A cry escaped her lips, and she bit down hard on her lower lip. He'd barely begun to stimulate her, yet the waves relentlessly slammed into her. Over and over. More and more intense until she could keep silent no longer. She screamed. He covered her mouth with his, while he continued using his fingers to prolong the orgasm until she finally pushed him away.

He trailed his lips from her mouth to her jaw, down to her breasts, laving each nipple and then going lower. When he got to her navel she stopped him. "Get the condom," she ordered, stunned at the level of her sensitivity. "Please."

Clint rolled over, grabbed his wallet out of his jeans' pocket and produced a blue foil packet. After ripping it open, he handed the package to her. Heat flamed in her chest and climbed her neck. He obviously wanted her to do the honors. What would he think if she admitted she'd never done it before? Heck, it couldn't be difficult. She removed the condom, placed it on the glistening crown and carefully unrolled the rubber down his hard penis.

"You trying to kill me?"

She froze. "What?"

His grimace turned into a lopsided smile. "You go any slower and I'm gonna have heart failure."

"Oh." She quickly finished the job.

He wasted no time in urging her onto her back and using his bent leg to spread her thighs. She mentally readied herself for his entry and was startled when he touched her with his hand.

"Nice. You're still wet for me."

His frankness embarrassed her. She didn't know why, she was twenty-seven, for heaven's sake, but she'd only been intimate with two other men. "Are you going to talk about it or—"

He drove into her. Hard, and so fast, she couldn't breathe. Instinctively, she wrapped her legs around his waist, lifting her fanny to meet each of his thrusts. After a few seconds, he slowed down, his shoulders quivering with restraint as he brushed the hair away from her damp cheek. "Ah, Dory."

"You trying to kill me?" she asked breathlessly. "Go any slower and—"

With three hard thrusts, he finished the job.

CLINT STARED UP AT the blue sky, content and relaxed with Dory's cheek pressed to his chest, his arm around her. He knew they had to get back to the barbecue, if for no other reason than Kate would be worried about her friend. But if he had his druthers, he'd stay right here with her naked body curled against his. Then, too, returning had its pluses. He'd only had one condom with him but in his nightstand there was a whole box.

He wondered what her reaction would be if he voiced his thoughts. Sweet, sweet Dory. A jack of all trades except when it came to sex. Her obvious lack of experience had really touched him. Pleased him far more than it should. She probably had some crazy text-book explanation about his Neanderthal roots, about a man's possessive desire to conquer his woman. Made Clint smile.

Hard to believe she'd only be here two more nights. He hoped she planned on spending them in his room and not the guest room. Selfishly, he even hated that he had to share her with his sister. He really did want to show her more of the Sugarloaf, maybe even bounce some ideas off her. She might not know about the daily workings of a ranch, but she was smart and had common sense. If he was off base on the changes he wanted to make, he could count on her to tell him the truth.

He heard her sigh, felt her warm breath dance across his skin, and damned if he wasn't turned on again. "Hey."

"Hmm." She sounded sleepy and snuggled closer.

"You're leaving on Monday, aren't you?"

She looked up at him with wary brown eyes, and nodded.

He kissed her forehead. "Any chance you can stay longer?"

Regret transformed her features. "I have to work."

"I figured." He shrugged, disappointed, but not surprised. Why did she have to live so damn far away? "Will you be staying in Honolulu for a while, or are you headed back to Cambodia?"

"No plans to go to Asia in the near future. My assignment there is done for now." She settled again on his chest, her face averted. "Why?"

He cleared his throat. "I don't know. You ever come to the mainland for work?"

"Rarely, though sometimes for a conference or maybe to speak at a seminar."

"How long a flight is it from Honolulu, anyway?" This was nuts. He'd never once had trouble with women. Why didn't he just come out and tell her he wanted to see her again?

"To Houston a direct flight is about eight hours." She'd tensed, her finger nervously swirling an abstract pattern on his chest. "Ever been to Hawaii?"

"Can't say that I have."

They let silence lapse.

"I wouldn't mind going if I had someone to show me around," he said finally, and felt her smile against his chest.

She brought her head up. "Lucky for you I'm an excellent guide. I even know some choice skinny-dipping spots on Maui."

He raised a brow in mock disapproval. "*You* go skinny-dipping?"

"No." She lightly pinched his nipple. "But I know where the private waterfalls are. Anyway, what's wrong with skinny-dipping? You forget I grew up around a bunch of hippies."

He grinned. "I think I'd like to meet your parents."

"Oh, God." She collapsed on his chest.

"Why not?" he asked, laughing. "You know my family."

She stayed perfectly still, almost as if she were afraid to move. "We'll see."

He stared up at the sky, aware of what she was thinking. Once the weekend was over and she'd left, would he still think about her? Would he make that long flight to Hawaii? He understood her doubt, but he knew without question that he wanted to see Dory again.

"Guess we should be getting back," she said, "before they send a posse out for us."

"Nah, the posse is half in the bag by now." He checked his watch. "But we do have to go, or Kate'll string me up."

Dory sat up, yawned and stretched, her bare beasts taunting him. "Hmm…I've never been to a lynching."

Unable to resist, he suckled one of her lush pink nipples. "You're damn lucky I don't have another condom with me."

APPARENTLY NO ONE had missed them. The chili cook-off had run late, and Kate had spent most of the day in the kitchen supervising dinner preparations. Dory hadn't seen Lisa at all, but she'd spotted Jessica sparring with a tall, good-looking cowboy, who Dory learned was an old friend of Joe and Clint's. That was going to be an interesting story when they all got together for their gab session later. The thought stopped Dory, made her consider how much she wanted to spill about Clint.

The problem wasn't just that he was Kate's brother. It went deeper. Not only did Dory simply not do one-night stands, she'd never been with a guy like Clint. Oh, yeah, he was hot, off-the-charts hot, but it wasn't that, either. He was a genuinely good man. He cared about his family, the ranch, the land, and as a lover he'd been selfless. That had really surprised her because in her experience, guys like him could take and take and they'd always have a woman willing to give.

Still, would he make an effort to see her again? She believed that he believed they would reconnect. She was certain he hadn't been feeding her a line of bull. But once she was out of sight, would she be out of mind, as well? And what about her? That was easy. Memories of the few hours they'd shared would stay with her for the rest of her life.

People had lined up for the chicken and ribs coming off the grills. Clint had a word with Pete, while she got them each a beer, and then, agreeing they weren't hungry yet, they sat in front of the stage while the band played an old country song.

"I think I'll grab a shower before the dance starts." Clint surprised her by how close he sat, by how often he touched her.

"Oh, no, the dance. I forgot."

"It'll be fun." He grinned. "And crowded."

"Meaning no one would miss us if we weren't there?" she asked, shaking her head at the devilish glint in his eyes.

"I like a smart woman."

She elbowed him, and noticed an attractive twenty-something blonde staring at them peevishly. It wasn't the first time. Dory had seen other women staring, either enviously or in disbelief, and even though she knew she should leave it alone, she had to ask. "Clint? Why me?"

"Why you, what?"

"There are so many totally gorgeous women here today. Something tells me you could've had your pick."

He got serious. "You're every bit as pretty, smarter than most, no, probably smarter than all of them, and you're the first woman who was interested enough to ask what I wanted in life. Answer enough?"

She smiled, her heart swelling at his earnestness. So what that he'd lied about her being just as pretty. She liked that he defended her. "Which reminds me, you blew off my question earlier. What are you going to do about implementing your ideas for the ranch? I'm sure you can persuade Joe to see reason."

"No, you owe me an answer first. Why me?"

That startled a laugh out of her. Was he kidding? "Well, because you're hot."

He looked equally startled, and then the corners of his mouth twitched as he tried not to smile. "That's shallow, and I'm hurt."

"You'll get over it. Come win me a teddy bear."

"Ah, hell, you probably can outshoot me," he grumbled.

"How about if I promise not to show you up?"

"Deal." He got up first, and then pulled her to her feet, trapping her between the bench and his body. "Throw in a kiss."

"Here?" She swallowed, afraid to see who might be watching.

"Chicken," he whispered.

She hesitated. "Clint."

He coaxingly brushed his lips over hers. "I believe it's what you anthropologists would call marking my territory."

Smiling, she looped her arms around his neck. "You're really awful."

"But hot."

"Yes," she agreed, laughing. And smart and fun and full of surprises. But she'd wait until he got to Hawaii to admit it.

WILD AT HEART

1

YE GODS, WAS TEXAS always this hot? Jessica Meade hobbled over the uneven ground to the kitchen door, wiped her face with the towel draped around her neck and guzzled water from a bottle she'd left on the steps. She'd only been out for a lousy twenty minutes but it felt like an hour. Although she had planned on cutting her morning run short so that she could have a cup of coffee alone with Kate, and then call her office in New York.

This wasn't the best time for her to be away from the magazine with the twentieth anniversary issue coming up next month, but she hadn't the heart to turn down Kate's invitation to her family's annual July Fourth celebration. It wasn't the festivities Jessica cared about, but the opportunity to see all three of her college roommates. Lisa and Dory had agreed to the reunion right away, and now that Kate had become engaged this might be their last chance before another five years slipped by.

Something furry scuttled under the steps, and Jessica froze until she realized it was only a harmless bunny. Behind her, she heard the distant low of grazing cows and the pounding of hooves as the hired hands headed out to the pastures. She'd never been to a ranch, or west of the Mississippi for that matter. With her being East

Coast born and bred, the Sugarloaf Ranch seemed as foreign to her as Asia.

But she was glad to be here because even though she and Kate talked on the phone twice a month, Jessica hadn't seen her since they'd graduated from college. And she knew as soon as Kate stepped out of the house yesterday to greet them, that something was wrong. A newly engaged woman should be glowing, not pale, tired-looking and in dire need of a hair trim.

The kitchen was buzzing with activity when she entered, regardless that it was only seven-thirty in the morning. Later in the afternoon was the big barbecue, and half a dozen women were busy making coleslaw, potato salad, baked beans and kneading dough for rolls. All of it just as foreign to Jessica as the ranch. With her busy schedule, if she couldn't call for a take-out salad or pop something frozen into the microwave, she simply didn't eat.

Kate wasn't there, but Jessica was assured by the housekeeper that Kate would return within the hour. Just enough time for her to call the office and shower, she decided, and made her way to her room. The log-cabin style house was enormous with several bedrooms upstairs belonging to Kate and her brothers, and four guest rooms downstairs. Nice, because no one had to share a room, however, her and Dory's rooms did adjoin to one bathroom.

She stopped outside her room, thinking she heard something inside, shrugged it off and opened the door. A tall, well-muscled man stood near the bed, rubbing his long wet sandy-blond hair with a towel. He was totally naked.

"Oh, my God. I'm so sorry. I—I thought this was my

room. Oh, God." She couldn't seem to move. Mortification kept her rooted to the spot.

He hooked the towel around his neck, surprise flickering in his blue eyes. And then a grin spread across his tanned face. "Don't be shy, darlin', come on in."

She gasped, stumbled backward and slammed the door shut. How could she have made such a stupid mistake? Her gaze darted down the hall as she counted the closed doors. There was Dory's room, and next to it the bathroom they shared. She blinked, slowly counted again. She hadn't made a mistake. This was her room. Who the hell was he?

She raised her hand to knock, but the image of his laughing blue eyes, broad shoulders, slim hips and… Stop. Stop. Stop. She couldn't go there. Couldn't think about *that* not even for a second. He obviously was a relative or friend of the Manning family. How could she ever look him in the eyes again? Or anywhere else.

Groaning, she concentrated on pulling herself together, waited a few seconds until she knew she wouldn't totally embarrass herself and then delivered three forceful knocks. Her heart raced erratically and every instinct told her to leave, let Kate iron out this mix-up. But it was too late. Suddenly disappearing would only make a future meeting with the man all the more awkward.

"Come in," he called.

"Are you decent?"

"That's a loaded question." His deep, rumbling laughter infused her with annoyance.

She'd turned to leave when the door opened.

Cautiously she slid him a glance. He'd pulled on jeans, zipped, but not snapped. His feet and chest were still bare, but she could handle that, even if he did have a remarkable chest.

He pushed the door wider and stepped back to allow her entrance.

She stayed where she was. "I believe this is my room."

"I don't think—" He frowned, looking sincerely perplexed. "You sure?"

Shifting so that she had a better look inside, she motioned with a nudge of her chin. "That's my suitcase there in the corner."

He twisted around, and she noticed a nasty scar slashed across his lower back. "Damn, I was so tired I didn't even notice it." He gave her a lopsided smile. "Sorry, darlin', Kate always puts me in here, but she wasn't around when I got in. You know where she's at?"

Jessica shook her head. Was this Kate's fiancé? The sudden stab of disappointment took Jessica aback. So what if he were? Except this man didn't look like a high school principal. Not with his longish hair and unshaven face. Or muscular physique and rugged tan. He looked more like an actor in a commercial touting the virtues of a Western vacation.

"You must be one of Kate's college friends from back East," he said, grabbing a blue T-shirt he'd tossed on the bed.

"Yes, I'm Jessica Meade." She gripped the water bottle as if it were life support, stunned that he could stand there casually talking as if she hadn't just seen him *naked.* Of course she was still embarrassed enough for the both of them.

"Ben Anderson." He pulled on the shirt and stifled a yawn. "Sorry. I drove most of the night."

"Oh." She shifted her weight, willing him to leave her room. "I don't know where Kate is."

"So you said." Amusement lit his eyes as his gaze

roamed her face. "We don't have to mention any of this."

Thankfully, she wasn't one to blush, but the mortification was still there, making her tongue feel thick. "No."

"When I meet you later, I'll act like it's the first time." He patted his pockets and glanced around the room. "You see my keys anywhere?"

He obviously didn't give a rat's behind that he'd literally been caught with his pants down. In a way, his cockiness served her well. Annoyance was overtaking embarrassment.

"Over there." She pointed to the oak dresser. "Are you family or friend?" she asked, wondering how often she should expect to be bumping into him.

"Practically family. I've known the Mannings most of my life. Went to school with Kate's brothers, Clint and Joe."

"Ah." She tried not to stare at his chest.

"Let's see…now where did I put my duffel?" Pursing his lips, he stuffed his keys into his pocket as he surveyed the room, and then nodded. "The bathroom. Afraid I used up your nice clean towels. I'll go rustle up some fresh ones."

"You don't have to do that."

He sized her up, starting with her pasty white legs up to her damp clinging tank top. "You know where the linen closet is?"

"Uh, no."

His mouth curved in a faint smile. "I'll be right back."

"Seriously, I'll figure it—" She might as well have been talking to the wall. He disappeared down the hall, and she hurried into the bathroom to check her reflec-

tion. Good Lord. She couldn't have looked worse if
she'd worked at it all day.

The morning before she'd left Manhattan she'd paid
over a hundred bucks to freshen up her ash-blond high-
lights and now she looked as if she'd been caught in a
dust storm. Her hair hung in dark, limp ropes and traces
of mascara she hadn't removed last night had smeared
so badly her hazel eyes looked muddy.

She pulled back her hair, bent over the sink and
quickly scrubbed her face. Too late, she remembered
she had no towel. Her tank top wasn't too disgusting
so she yanked it up and dried off her face. With the
sickening feeling that someone was watching, she
turned to find Ben standing in the bathroom doorway.
Fortunately she wore a sports bra beneath the tank
top, which she calmly pulled back down over her
exposed belly.

Ben grinned and held out two folded towels. "Here
I thought you were returning the favor."

"Funny." She took the towels, picked up his duffel
and handed it to him. "Goodbye."

THE KITCHEN was more crowded than a bull chute during the annual Las Vegas rodeo. Maria, the housekeeper, had already threatened to put Ben to work if he
got in the way. He poured himself a third cup of coffee,
trying to wake up. All he wanted to do was crawl into
a nice soft bed with an even softer pillow and clean
sheets that weren't motel issue.

Normally he wouldn't have pushed so hard, driving
twelve hours straight through as he had last night after
riding in the Sun Valley rodeo, but it couldn't be helped.
Not if he'd wanted to make it here for the Mannings'
Fourth of July bash. He hadn't missed one yet, even

though it had cost him some substantial prize money over the years.

None of it mattered now. He stretched out his neck, getting a good twist out of his shoulder, and heard his back crack. There wasn't going to be much bareback riding left in his future. Age and injuries were a bitch.

Maria slid a plate onto the butcher-block island. It was an egg and sausage burrito she knew he liked. "Sit and eat," she told him, and when he started to protest that he didn't want to be any trouble, she held up a plump hand. "Don't argue."

"I don't know why you won't give in and marry me, Maria." He grabbed her around the waist and kissed her creased cheek. "You know I'll keep asking till I've got one foot in the grave."

She gave him a shove and shook her graying head in mock frustration. The rest of the women laughed, most of them familiar with their long and playful relationship, and then went back to their chatting and gossip as they cooked for tonight.

Trying to stay out of the way, he stood in the corner while he wolfed down the burrito and sipped his coffee. Clint would probably need Ben's help outside, which is where he was headed as soon as he was done eating. In keeping with tradition, Joe, preferring to handle the ranch routine, wasn't likely to show up until dinner tonight.

Ben popped the last bite into his mouth and went to the sink to rinse out his cup when he realized the women's chattering had abruptly stopped. He glanced over his shoulder to see what that was about and saw her in the doorway. The petite woman he'd met earlier. Kate's friend, Jessica. She looked completely different, her hair up in a fancy twist, and dressed in pressed white slacks that were itching to get dirty, but it was her.

Apparently acknowledging their rude staring, the women turned back to their work, but not before exchanging amused glances. If Jessica noticed, she didn't let on. She brushed the shoulder of her blue silky blouse and briefly touched the fancy red, blue and gold scarf around her neck.

"Anyone know where Kate is?" she asked, a polite smile lifting her pink-tinted lips as her gaze swept the kitchen. When her eyes came to rest on him, her expression fell. She blinked, recovered, the smile returning to her face. "Hello again."

He couldn't resist, and gave her a questioning look. "Have we met?"

She narrowed her gaze, ever so slightly, but he didn't miss her warning.

He shrugged, doing his best to keep a straight face. "I told you I wouldn't say a word."

That pretty much piqued everyone's interest, and if a pin dropped someone could hear it clear on the other side of the house.

"I'm sorry I took so long." Kate came rushing in from the swinging dining room doors, her arms loaded with packages. "Oh, Ben, you're here. I was starting to worry."

"Let me get that." He kissed her cheek before taking the paper sacks. "What's wrong, Kate, you look flustered."

"I'm running late." She pointed to the counter near the pantry. "With everything. And I'm losing my mind."

As ordered, he set down the bags, which Maria immediately dived into. "Anything to do with that nasty rumor I heard?"

Her face creased in a puzzled frown.

"You getting married?"

Kate's features tightened. "I can't even think about that right now." She caught sight of Jessica standing near the hall, and sighed. "We were supposed to have coffee. I'm sorry."

"It's okay." Jessica stepped forward. "Let me help."

Kate eyed her fancy getup with a troubled frown. "I could use it."

"Anything you want, sweetie."

Kate turned to Ben. "How about you two run into town for me?"

2

JESSICA CRINGED. The last thing she wanted to do was get stuck within the confines of a car with Ben. "Maybe you could use my help here and Ben can run into town on his own," she suggested mildly.

Kate's eyebrows shot up. "If it came to that, I suspect Ben would be of more use in the kitchen than you. No offense. Unless you've finally learned to cook."

"I know how to cook." In college she hadn't had time with her full course load and two part-time jobs. "I just don't do much of it."

"I wouldn't either if I could get the kind of takeout you get in Manhattan." Kate glanced down at Jessica's pink toenails, peeking out from her white high-heeled sandals. She brought her head up, smiled and then slid a look at Ben. "Where are my manners? Have you two met?"

"Yes," Jessica said at the same time Ben said, "No."

Kate chuckled. "Okay." She glanced at the wall clock, her brows furrowing. "Ben, you have time to drive to town?"

"Sure."

"Jessica, can I have a quick word with you?" she asked, and Jessica nodded, then followed her into the hall, her heels clicking noisily on the wood floor.

Kate kept her voice low but didn't mince words. "I hope you brought jeans."

Jessica made a face. "Actually, I didn't." She sighed. "This trip was last-minute and I didn't have time to shop."

"I know." Kate gave her a quick hug. "I'm glad you could make it. I am, but I want you to be comfortable and not ruin your good clothes. Obviously I can't help you because I'm so much taller than you."

"No problem. I'm sure I can find at least one pair of jeans in town that fit, and I have my running shoes."

A loud crash came from the kitchen.

Kate briefly closed her eyes and rubbed her right temple. "Not one of my better days," she murmured, backing up. "Did I tell you that you look great? So incredibly glamorous."

"We'll have to find some time to talk," Jessica said.

"We will, I promise." And then Kate disappeared through the door.

A moment later, Ben stuck his head out. "Kate's writing out a list. My truck's near the stables. Go change and I'll meet you out back."

On her way to her room, Jessica loosened the scarf and yanked it off. Why was everyone so damn worried about how she was dressed? And anyway, what did she know about casual ranch attire? Sure she was fashion editor for the magazine but that applied to style for *normal* people.

She left the scarf lying across the dresser and grabbed her purse. No point in changing her clothes as Ben had suggested. All she could do was exchange her linen slacks for another pair because that's all she'd brought. She didn't own anything more casual because she didn't need it, not with working thirteen-hour days. Any free time she eked out, she spent sleeping or crashed on the couch studying a competitor's magazine.

Besides, it was nice to have the luxury of owning designer clothes. In college Kate had always dressed fashionably. Lisa had the enviable knack of looking casually chic no matter what she wore. But of course, like Kate, she'd had a hefty wardrobe allowance. Dory's folks had money, too, but Dory had always been more comfortable in jeans. Jessica had never had a choice.

She'd secretly shopped at thrift stores, because even though her scholarship covered most of her education, her part-time job afforded no money for frills or entertainment. Her single mother barely made ends meet and she hadn't dared ask her for a penny. Luckily, those days were over, Jessica's hard work had paid off, and she enjoyed a privileged lifestyle.

As soon as she rounded the front of the house, she knew she would have been better off leaving through the kitchen. Ben stood clear across the huge backyard, waiting next to a dusty red pickup truck. Knowing it was useless to hope that wasn't their mode of transportation, she still cringed when he opened the door. Maybe the inside was cleaner than the outside and her poor white slacks wouldn't be totally ruined.

She hadn't changed her heels, which was really dumb she realized as she gingerly picked her way over the rocky ground, watching carefully where she took each step. All she needed was to have to board the plane home on crutches. As she got closer, she looked up.

Ben was leaning on the truck's open door, shaking his head. "You're crazy, you know that?"

"Excuse me?" she said with a haughty lift of her chin. Naturally she knew what he was talking about, but she wouldn't give him the satisfaction of admitting to her stupidity. Besides, she really needed to concentrate on where she was walking.

He came toward her suddenly, eating up the distance between them in loose, long-legged strides. "You're gonna break your pretty little neck," he said, picking her up and throwing her over his shoulder.

At first she was too stunned to object. She stared down at the ground, at the curve of his butt, well aware that the side of her ass scraped against his stubbly jaw with each bumpy step he took.

"Put me down," she ground out, twisting, arching her back, and feeling his hold tighten around her thighs.

"Hold on now, damn it, before you punt the family jewels." The words were barely out of his mouth when she made contact with her toes, and he grunted, muttering, "Just what I was trying to avoid."

As angry as she was, she really didn't want to injure him. She stilled her legs and clenched her teeth at the indignity, the few moments it took to get to the truck feeling like an eternity. He set her on her feet, and she glared up at him in outraged disbelief, words escaping her.

"You're the one asking for trouble, darlin'," he said, grimacing and briefly cupping his crotch. "Walking around out here with those skinny heels, you're just begging to end up in a cast." He opened the passenger door for her.

She snorted. Did he seriously think she'd go anywhere with him now? With the sun shining in his face, his light eyes were a startling shade of blue, and his square jaw was softened by a deep cleft in the middle of his chin. Not that his good looks excused his behavior, or tempted her to change her mind....

A heavy swatch of hair fell to her left shoulder. Her hand flew to her carefully sculpted French twist. It was lopsided and loose. Damn it.

"Come on. You can fix your hair in the truck." He

motioned with an impatient hand. "Kate is going batty enough as it is. We don't need to take all day getting her stuff in town."

The truth of that softened Jessica. Her pride wasn't worth stressing Kate out any further. She grabbed on to the door handle for support. The truck was a monster, high enough off the ground that she'd have to hoist herself up.

"Need some help?" he offered with an extended hand, his palm large and callused.

"No, thank you." She briefly eyed the seat, saw that it was remarkably clean and pulled herself up. Though it wasn't easy in heels, she decided she'd rather land on her backside than accept his help.

She watched him round the hood and then climb in behind the wheel. Sitting on the seat between them was a black cowboy hat that he picked up and set on his head before inserting the key and starting the engine. Now that she wasn't worried about falling on her ass or staring into his eyes, she noticed that he'd changed his T-shirt to a Western-cut tan shirt with the sleeves rolled back. On the foot pressing the accelerator was a pointy black cowboy boot.

Settling back, she smiled, thinking about how he'd actually "dressed up" to go to town. And then she abruptly remembered that her French twist was askew and pulled down the passenger visor.

He directed them onto the gravel road leading to the highway and glanced over at her. "What are you looking for?"

"A mirror."

"Don't have one."

"I see that." She slapped the visor back in place. "I thought all cars had one there," she grumbled, rifling through her purse. She knew she had a mirror in there, just not one as big or convenient as she wanted.

"What did you bring an overnight bag for?"

She turned to see if he were teasing. He looked confused. "It's a purse."

"Biggest one I ever saw."

"You live a sheltered life." She found her mirror and a brush. Propping her purse on her lap, she placed the mirror just so. Her hands freed, she tried to repair the French twist without starting over but quickly saw that wasn't going to happen.

Annoyed, she yanked out the pins, let the rest of her hair fall to her shoulders and furiously dragged the brush through the thick locks. It was going to take her forever to get it just right again, she thought as she gathered the weight of her hair at her nape.

They went over a particularly nasty bump and half the pins she'd left on her lap scattered to the floor. She muttered a mild oath, which promptly garnered Ben's attention.

"Don't do that," he said, his gaze swinging from her to the road and back to her. "Leave it down."

She gave a dismissive wave of her hand. "You just worry about watching the road."

"I've got forty miles to do that."

"Good grief. The town is forty miles away?"

"This here is Texas, darlin'. Lots of wide-open spaces. Hell, the Mannings' spread alone takes up nearly fifteen miles to town."

She knew the ranch was big, and profitable, thanks to Kate's older brother, who'd stepped in to run things when their parents were killed in an accident. "Where's your ranch?"

"I don't have one. My folks used to own a much

smaller place with about a hundred acres west of here. But they sold it two years ago and moved to Tulsa to be close to my sister and her kids."

"Then what do you do?"

A slow smile lifted the corner of his mouth. "Rodeo."

She waited for further explanation and received silence. "Rodeo? I don't understand."

"I follow the rodeo circuit."

"So you're like a rider?"

One of his eyebrows went up. "Something like that."

She was obviously missing something. "Sorry, I don't know anything about the rodeo. It's not a hobby, I take it."

The corners of his mouth twitched. "I make my living off the prize money."

"Oh." She didn't want to sound nosy so went back to fixing her hair. But she was curious. He looked to be about thirty, and if he'd gone to school with Kate's brothers he had to be at least that. "I'm assuming you're not married."

"No." The way he shook his head and drew out the word said more than the word itself.

Maybe he was divorced. "Ever been?"

"Once." He frowned thoughtfully. "Can't remember her name, though."

Jessica swore she hadn't heard right. "Are you trying to be funny? Because you missed the mark by a mile."

"Don't get your hackles up." He kept his face straight ahead but looked suspiciously as if he were silently laughing at her. "We were only married for about twenty-four hours."

She sighed. "You're pulling my leg."

"Nope. It happened in Vegas. I'd just won the saddle bronc championship. I was, drunk." He shrugged. "She probably was, too. Who knows?"

She stared in mute disgust. She knew far too many guys like him. The kind she'd gone to high school with, or ones her brothers hung out with back in Philly. They worked their factory jobs during the day, and spent their paychecks in the bars and strip clubs at night. It didn't seem to matter if they had a wife and kids at home or not. Their ambition seemed to end with their first drink.

"Hey, I'm not proud of my behavior. It happened a long time ago when I was young and stupid."

"When? Last year?"

"Twelve years ago, for your information," he said, sounding irritated. "I was twenty, and I let the big win go to my head. Sorry I didn't have some fancy education like you to cushion my life."

Jessica bit her lip. Shame on her for being judgmental. It sounded as if Ben hadn't come from much, either. She'd been lucky to make it out of her neighborhood. That didn't give her the right to look down her nose at others. "I apologize," she said, busying herself with her hair. "Please forgive me."

He slid her a sidelong glance. "Make it up to me," he said with a ghost of a grin. "Leave your hair down."

3

BEN FOUND a parking space right in front of Wilbur's Food Town. Next to the small grocery store was Porter's Sport and Sundry, where Jessica would be able to pick up a pair of jeans and some decent shoes. If she struck out there, he'd give in and drive the extra thirty miles to Willowville, where they had a medium-size department store. He hoped they wouldn't need to do that because they didn't have much time. The list of supplies Kate had given him were for the chili cook-off, which was to begin in roughly two hours. Odd, how disorganized Kate seemed this year. Probably had her mind on her upcoming wedding.

He got out of the truck, and then watched Jessica carefully slide down from the passenger side onto the sidewalk. She was a tiny little thing, prickly, too. Without the high heels, he'd guess she was maybe five-two, almost a foot shorter than him.

Once she seemed sure of her footing, she pulled the large black leather bag along with her. A purse. Hell, the thing was almost as big as his duffel.

"If we split up we can save time." He pulled Kate's list out of his back pocket, his gaze catching on Jessica's prissy high-heeled sandals. "Unless you need my help choosing something appropriate."

She pressed her pretty pink lips together, her hazel

eyes turning a fiery shade of gold, and then said, "I'll see you in a few minutes."

The grocery list was sizable, but Ben took much less time to gather the groceries than he'd expected thanks to two helpful young clerks he vaguely remembered. After he stowed the bags of goods in the truck, he went into Porter's to look for Jessica. She was coming out of one of the dressing rooms to use the store's only full-length mirror when he found her.

She didn't see him, so he hung back and watched as she studied her reflection with a critical eye. The jeans she had on were a couple of inches too long but they were a nice snug fit that showed off her curvy hips and rounded rear end. The striped shirt was okay, not especially feminine. In fact, she might have found it in the boy's section. Maybe the store's limited selection was the problem.

He looked at her feet and saw that she still had on the high-heeled sandals. Hell, he hoped this wasn't as far as she'd gotten the whole time he was next door. On a display shelf he saw a handsome pair of women's snakeskin boots and picked them up.

Just as he approached her, a young woman came out of the dressing room with a mess of clothes hung over her arm and a disgruntled expression on her face.

"What other colors do you have these jeans in?" Jessica asked, while twisting around to check out her reflection from the back.

Ben chuckled, snagging the attention of both women. "Jeans come in different colors now? What'll they think of next?"

Jessica snubbed him, and turned to the blonde salesclerk.

"Ben?" A wide grin spread across the younger

woman's flushed face. "I knew you'd be here for the rodeo, but I didn't expect to see you in town."

He remembered her, she was Frank Miller's daughter, but Ben couldn't recall her name. He removed his hat and nodded to her. She wasn't wearing a name tag. Around here everyone knew everybody else. "Kate sent me over to Wilbur's for a few things. How's your dad doing?"

"He's sold off most of the heifers. Took it in his head to start raising Arabians." She rolled her eyes. "You know him…always looking for another way to make my brothers crazy." She dumped the load of clothes onto a chair and gave a flirty toss of her straw-like hair. "I heard you made it to the Montana Circuit finals. That's a tough one."

"Yep. About six months ago." He didn't like thinking about Montana. A few years ago he wouldn't have just made the finals. He would've won the whole damn thing. But after that last fall he was gun-shy, and according to the doctors, for damn good reason. "You still in school?"

"Oh, for heaven's sakes. I left community college two years ago. I never did have much of a head for school." Her gaze lowered to his belt buckle. "That's a new one."

"Uh, excuse me, Crystal," Jessica interrupted in a crisp no-nonsense tone.

Crystal Miller. That was it.

She responded to Jessica with an annoyed look.

"We're rather limited on time," Jessica said. "Perhaps you two can catch up later. Now, about the jeans…"

"Around here, honey, jeans are jeans. If you wanted a crazy color like green or purple, *perhaps,*" she said, mimicking Jessica, "you should have brought them with you." And then with an eye roll only he could see, she returned her attention to Ben, her rudeness shocking. "You know you're gonna have to save me a dance tonight." She winked. "Maybe show me your new buckle up close."

God, she made him feel old. He had ten, eleven years on her at least, although not long ago that wouldn't have mattered to him. He would've accepted her not-so-subtle invitation without a second thought. "Jessica is right. We are in a hurry to take Kate her groceries."

Crystal's eyes widened. "You're together?" She didn't seem anxious to look Jessica's way. Instead, she bent to collect the clothes she'd dropped on the chair.

"I'll take these jeans," Jessica said, not sounding the least bit perturbed by Crystal's earlier attitude. "Two pairs if you have them." She frowned at her reflection. "I guess this shirt will do. Better than ruining one of my good blouses."

"I'll go check for another size four." Crystal seemed relieved to disappear into the front of the store.

Ben noticed a cute yellow sundress hanging on a rack outside the dressing room door and pointed to it. "You try that on?"

Jessica snorted. "Why would I?"

"For the dance."

The patronizing curve of Jessica's lips ignited a spark of irritation in his belly. "Not my style." She looked pointedly at the pair of boots in his hand. "What are those?"

"Not bad, huh?"

"What are you, my personal shopper?"

He shook his head. "You are the most fickle female I've ever met."

"Okay, I'm sorry. I know we don't have much time and you're trying to help." She took the boots to examine them. "The thing is, I'd probably never wear them again."

He saw her glance at the price. Without looking, he knew they were expensive. Was that stopping her? As little experience as he had with women's clothes, he knew the ones she wore weren't cheap. Then it occurred to him he didn't know anything about her, other than she lived in New York and she was Kate's college friend.

"Ah, they probably aren't even your size," he said, taking the boots from her, unsettled by the sudden irrational desire to see her wearing them with those snug little jeans.

She thoughtfully wrinkled her nose. "Actually, they are."

"I've got another pair of size-four jeans," Crystal said, cutting in as she swept toward the dressing area, her smile conciliatory. "And this denim blouse is kind of cute."

Jessica didn't share her opinion, judging by the reluctance in her eyes. "I'm only going to be here two more days. I think I'm all right." She checked her watch, and asked Crystal to wrap up her purchases while she changed.

Ben waited until she was in the dressing room before he handed the boots to Crystal. "I'll take these," he said, and reached into his back pocket for his wallet. "But do me a favor and don't say anything to the lady."

BEN INSISTED that he could unload the groceries by himself, so Jessica carried her packages to her room. She'd cut off the tags from the jeans she'd tried on at the store and worn them home. Even with the heels on they were too long and she'd had to cuff them. It would be worse with her running shoes but she didn't care. She had more important things on her mind. Like how to squash the recurring images popping into her mind of Ben naked.

Even if she hadn't seen what a fine specimen he was in the raw, she had to acknowledge that he was a very good-looking man. Not in a classic way—he had more of a rugged, earthy charm that she'd never have guessed would appeal to her. From reactions in town she'd gathered that he was a pretty big deal with the whole rodeo thing. She'd have to subtly find out from Kate what that was about.

She finished changing, decided to leave her hair down because it was convenient and not because Ben had asked, and then went to find Kate. She was in the kitchen, doing an inventory of the ingredients for the chili cook-off.

"Isn't that much better?" Kate said when she saw her. "I'm glad they had your size in town." Her gaze went to the cuffs. "I have a sewing machine."

"This is fine." Jessica's gaze strayed out the kitchen window toward the barn where the booths and tents were set up. People had already shown up for the day's festivities, kids mostly, but there were a few ranch hands milling about. She didn't see Ben, though.

"I think he went to see if Clint needs help."

Jessica snapped her gaze to Kate. "Who?"

Her friend smiled knowingly. "Sorry, my mistake."

"I wasn't looking for Ben. I had quite enough of him during that trip to town."

Kate stopped what she was doing to stare at Jessica. "Did something happen?"

"Not really. But come on, sweetie, the guy really is full of himself." The words were no sooner out of her mouth when shame washed over her. They weren't true, and she had no idea why she'd made such an unfair statement.

Kate's mouth dropped open.

"I shouldn't have said that." Jessica glanced around

at the other women, who fortunately were too busy to have heard.

Concern clouded Kate's eyes, and she ushered Jessica out the door to the privacy of the hall. "Granted, this isn't the best time in Ben's life, but acting full of himself doesn't seem at all like him. Please tell me what happened."

"Nothing. Honestly." Jessica sighed. "We started out on the wrong foot, and some of it was my fault. All right, maybe even most of it." She thought about him naked, about how he'd carried her to the truck and how strong and solid he'd felt beneath her. "He was trying to be helpful."

A mixture of curiosity and amusement sparkled in Kate's eyes. "*Et tu,* Jessica? I wouldn't have guessed."

"What does that mean?"

"Were the girls in town being totally silly? Some of those buckle bunnies can really be annoying. But considering he's a local hero and hot, he handles it pretty well."

"Well, I don't think he's hot, and I don't know anything about the hero thing. And what the hell is a buckle bunny?"

Kate chuckled. "A rodeo groupie. And believe me, Ben's got plenty of them. You're probably the only female in five hundred miles who doesn't think he's attractive. Look, I've got to get back to the kitchen."

"Wait." Jessica hesitated, not wanting her friend to get the wrong impression, yet she was far too curious not to ask. "What did you mean about this not being the best time in Ben's life?"

Now Kate looked hesitant. "The rodeo has been his life. Watching his career end at thirty-two can't be easy."

From the kitchen, the housekeeper called to Kate.

"I've got to go." She squeezed Jessica's arm. "Don't say anything to him, okay?"

"Of course not." She followed Kate, but her thoughts stayed with Ben. How awful for him. Although she didn't understand why he was faced with this dilemma at such a young age. "What can I do now?"

Kate glanced at her watch. "In a few minutes you can help Ben register the cook-off contestants."

Jessica started to protest. She didn't think it a good idea to spend any more time with Ben. Not when she couldn't seem to stop picturing those six-pack abs, the contour of muscle bulging from his thighs, the impressively long and thick...

Another thought registered with sickening clarity.

"Damn it." She hadn't realized she'd spoken out loud until all the women in the kitchen turned to stare.

How could she have forgotten to call her office?

4

"WELL, LET'S SEE." Ben studied the clipboard with all the seriousness of a teacher grading a final exam. "Looks to me like one of the Wilson sisters is a no-show. That leaves us with only fourteen contestants this year."

"Thirteen." Jessica held up two numbered cards that were linked to two contestants, thereby keeping the submissions anonymous until they could be judged later in the afternoon. "We seem to have two no-shows."

"Nope. One of those is mine."

She laughed. "*You're* entering the chili cook-off?"

"Damn straight. Who do you think came in first place four years out of the last five?"

"No way."

He tried to look offended. "I've got the blue ribbons to prove it."

"Who does the judging?"

"I don't like your tone or your implication, darlin'," he said lazily. "I explained before that the contest is anonymous. I've won fair and square."

"I meant no disrespect to the big winner." Holding her hands up in supplication, she bit back a smile. "Is it too late for me to enter? I could take the place of the no-show."

"I thought you didn't cook."

"A nasty rumor. I assure you, I make a mean chili."

He lifted a skeptical brow. "Where did you say you're from?"

"Philly. Philadelphia," she corrected. "And yes, we eat chili there, too. What's the matter? Afraid of the competition?"

"Competition?" He hooted with laughter. "I just don't want to see you humiliated, is all."

She snatched the remaining contestant's card. "We'll see."

"Well, now, if you're so sure of yourself, how about we make a small wager?" He grinned devilishly. "Just between us."

The image of him naked popped into her head. She swallowed, cleared her throat. "What did you have in mind?"

"It's always winner's choice."

"What if neither of us wins?"

His mouth curved in a cocky smile, and he tugged down his hat to shadow his eyes. "Don't you worry your pretty little head about that."

"You're right. It was temporary insanity to underestimate myself like that." She fisted her hair and lifted it off the back of her neck. The weather was far too warm for her hair to be down. She'd have to pin it up while she cooked. "What time do we start?"

He didn't have a chance to answer. A trio of adoring young women approached and started chatting him up. Jessica swore he had the largest fan club outside of Hollywood. For the past forty minutes he'd been bombarded with sweet young things vying for his attention. He'd always been polite and charming, though not necessarily eager to prolong the exchanges.

"Nice seeing you ladies again," he said after a few minutes, "but I've got to get to work on my chili."

The disappointment evident in their faces, they ambled off toward the game booths.

Jessica watched with amusement as he pretended not to see another of his admirers bearing down on him from the direction of the food tent.

"We best get our pots and ingredients before everyone has a head start on us," he said, and ducked under the counter to exit the booth.

Jessica followed, and saw the other contestants already setting up stoves in their respective booths, which consisted of poles holding up canvas canopies for shade. Some of them obviously took the cook-off seriously, and although space was limited and required sharing, territories were clearly marked. Signs with catchy names had been hooked to the poles, along with corny decorations and corresponding props serving as dividers.

The supply shed was well organized, offering a variety of canned goods, everything from stewed tomatoes to jalapeños and some weird items she'd never dreamed of putting in chili. There was also an assortment of spices from which to choose, although she learned that most people had their own secret ingredients. She also quickly discovered that hamburger wasn't automatically the meat of choice. Available to the contestants were venison, ground buffalo, ground turkey, pheasant and cubed steak.

She'd never eaten game meat before and tried not to show her instinctive disdain. One thing for sure, she didn't think she'd be sampling the other contestants' entries as it was apparently customary for everyone to do.

There were two large pots left, one each for her and

Ben, and she found it hilarious how secretive he was about collecting his ingredients. She took her brown paper sack and quickly threw in what she figured she needed, and then waited with her back turned while he finished his "shopping."

"You didn't have to wait for me," he said, eyeing her suspiciously as he emerged from the shed.

"I didn't know where to go."

"Right." He scanned the row of cooks, busy lighting their hot plates or already dumping ingredients into their pots. "Looks like we're left with the two on the end."

She followed him, seeing that both were occupied, and was surprised at the disappointment she felt that they wouldn't be sharing a spot. Still, they were just across from one another, and the truth was, they probably wouldn't have a minute to talk, not with his string of female groupies that seemed to sniff him out no matter where he was.

They stopped at the first booth, and Ben introduced her to the couple who was busy chopping onions and using a mortar and pestle to grind their own spices. The woman seemed mildly disappointed that they had to share their space, but she was pleasant and even helped Jessica get her Sterno lit without burning down the canopy.

Within ten minutes, Jessica had her meat and onions browned, and had emptied all her other ingredients into the pot to simmer. She looked over at the next booth, where Ben was still chopping and grinding. She couldn't help but smile at the picture he made in his white chef's apron and tall black Stetson, his expression absurdly serious.

He stopped to take a pull of beer and caught her

watching him. Frowning, he moved so that his broad body blocked her view and she couldn't see what he was doing. She laughed out loud, getting a funny look from her booth mates.

Ben's amused gaze went to her pot. "You're finished?"

"It has to simmer for two hours."

"This isn't even sporting. I'm gonna feel bad collecting on my bet." With one finger, he pushed up the rim of his hat, his eyes gleaming mischievously. "That's not to say I won't."

"Isn't there a country saying about not counting your chickens before they're hatched?"

He grinned. "If all you're doing is waiting, then come on over here, Philly, and let me show you a thing or two about making real honest-to-goodness chili."

"After all your secret voodoo moves over there, you're suddenly willing to tutor me? This better not be a trick to sabotage my entry," she said, tossing aside her apron.

It was ridiculous how her heart fluttered just because he'd asked her to join him. She hadn't hung out with the popular crowd in high school, she'd been too busy studying, yearning for that scholarship that would get her out of her shabby Philly neighborhood. But right now, she felt as if she were back in school and the captain of the football team had singled her out.

For good measure, she gave her chili another stir, and then walked the few feet to where he was putting some meat he'd chopped into his pot. The older man sharing Ben's booth smiled at Jessica, offered to get more beer and then headed for the refreshment tent, leaving them alone.

"I never asked you," Ben said. "What do you do?"

"I work for *TREND*." At his blank expression, she added, "It's a women's magazine." And because she couldn't resist, "I'm the food editor."

He froze, his jaw slackened, cupping a handful of minced onions midway to the pot.

She grinned. "Just kidding. I'm the fashion editor."

"Hell, I shouldn't have been fooled even for a minute."

"Keep it up, and you'll be eating a side of crow along with my winning chili."

"You've got spunk, I'll give you that." He moved close enough to her to make her pulse race, and then leaned past her to grab the cutting board.

"I'm in the way. I should go."

"No." He surprised her by putting a hand on her waist. "Don't." His warm moist breath danced across her cheek and for a heart-stopping instant, mingled with hers. "I won't tease you anymore."

"I don't care that you tease me."

His eyes truly were a remarkable shade of blue, almost spellbinding. His gaze fell briefly to her lips, and she tensed, fully expecting him to kiss her. Hoping desperately he would. But then he cleared his throat, glanced around and lowered his hand. "Pass me that spoon, will you?"

She blinked, trying to figure out what he'd said, and then pulling herself together, she twisted around to find the long-handled wooden spoon sitting on top of the sack of groceries. When she handed it to him, their eyes met. Her insides melted. It was clear that it didn't matter who won the bet. She knew how this would end.

WHAT BEN LIKED MOST about Jessica, he decided, as he sprinkled the last pinch of cayenne into the pot, was that she obviously didn't know squat about rodeoing. She didn't care about how many championships he'd racked up, or what was next on the circuit or how big the purse was.

She bent over to pick up a used paper sack to collect the empty cans, and his gaze riveted to her cute rear end. Okay, so maybe her lack of interest in the rodeo wasn't his favorite thing about her. Although not even the narrowness of her waist, the tempting swell of her breasts or the way she filled out those tight new jeans topped the list. Her sense of humor was a major turn-on, and how she'd been willing to roll with the punches and not get all prickly as he'd first assumed, were both way up there.

There was no question as to how he wanted the night to end, but the fact that she was Kate's friend could get sticky. He'd get in his truck and lay tracks this very second before he'd hurt Kate, or tick off Clint or Joe. Then again, he and Jessica were both adults and anything that happened between them shouldn't be anyone else's business. Theoretically, anyway.

There was still the matter of the boots he'd bought for her. He didn't know what the blazes had gotten into him. He just didn't do that kind of thing. If a woman he was dating asked for something, he never objected to providing the trinket, but he was never impulsive about gift-giving. Maybe he ought to return the boots, or give them to Kate to exchange for her size. He just couldn't picture himself handing them over to Jessica.

"You're going to stir that thing to death," she said, her hands on her curvy hips. "Don't tell me that's your secret to good chili."

With his mind on the boots, he had gotten carried away. He set the spoon aside and picked up his bottle of beer. "The trick is not letting the onions and garlic get too browned, just translucent and limp. And always use EVOO." He noticed her frown, and added, "Extra virgin olive oil."

Her brows arched in amusement. "Is that right?"

"Yep." He noticed the color of the onions and garlic wasn't what it should be, and he threw in another pinch of chili powder. "Bam!"

"Oh, my God." She looked as if she'd just won the lottery.

"What?"

"You watch the Food Network."

"The what?" Hiding his embarrassment, he gave her his back and stirred the pot again. Yeah, he'd watched Emeril and Rachel Ray a few times. Not much to do when you're stuck in a motel in between rodeos.

"Don't deny it. I've seen Emeril make that same move."

"Obviously, you watch all that crap."

"Crap?" She laughed gleefully. "I'm an insomniac. I watch cooking and design shows when I can't sleep. I've got no problem admitting that. How about you?"

"Okay, so I might have caught an episode or two when I've been channel surfing. But that doesn't need to go any further. You got that, Philly?"

She laughed again, looking far too smug.

"Hey, Ben."

Before he turned around he recognized the voice. Missy Thomas was the worst kind of buckle bunny. She was shameless and relentless, and he'd bet she'd slept with half the guys on the circuit, and it didn't seem to matter if they were married. He'd blown her off so many times he didn't know how to do it politely anymore. "Afternoon, Missy," he said, unsmiling.

"How long have you been back, Ben Anderson?"

Missy's long blond hair was tied into two pigtails and her blouse cut clear down to Tijuana. "Without calling me."

"Sorry, Missy." He slid an arm around Jessica and pulled her close to his side. There was a sure way of getting rid of Missy. "I've been busy," he said, and planted a kiss on Jessica's surprised mouth.

5

JESSICA AUTOMATICALLY put a hand on his chest to steady herself as he brushed his lips across hers, lingering at the corner of her mouth. Then he did this little nibbling thing that further elevated her dangerously high blood pressure.

He'd caught her completely off guard, and for a second she forgot that she was standing out in the open with a potential audience of fifty plus people. He felt wonderfully strong and solid beneath her palm, and she longed to explore further, to slip her fingers between the snaps of his shirt. She already knew she'd find a smooth, well-defined chest and dark tan nipples. Amazing how much detail she still recalled from such a brief glimpse of him this morning.

Ben pulled away first, and she was startled to discover that she'd continued to cling to him long past the point of necessity. He smiled down at her, and then kissed the top of her head before turning back to the blond woman.

"Sorry, Missy, what were you saying?"

"Nothing," she said with an abrupt lift of one shoulder and a dismissive toss of her head. "Break a leg tomorrow," she said sweetly, spun on her heel and headed toward a bunch of ranch hands drinking beer at a table near the stage.

"Why not? I've broken near everything else." Ben

stared after her, then he muttered nearly inaudibly, "That's one thing I won't miss."

Jessica stepped away a safe distance. "You were rude to her."

"I've tried every polite way I know how to let that young lady know I'm not interested. But she's pushy and stubborn and a damn—" He cut himself short, looking a bit sheepish. "Let's just say she's not much of a lady."

"So you thought it was okay to use me?"

He took off his hat and drove a hand through his hair, a stricken look on his face. "That wasn't exactly my intention."

Regretting her boorishness, she picked up the sack she'd discarded and started jamming in the empty cans. "You can't just kiss someone like that for no reason."

"Well, hell, it's not like I haven't wanted to kiss you all day." He set the hat back on his head and pulled the rim low. "And don't act like you didn't know it."

She glanced over her shoulder to make sure no one was listening. Fortunately, the older man sharing the booth had gone again.

"Or didn't want it," Ben added, his voice husky.

He was right, of course, but she didn't appreciate him pointing it out. She held his gaze. "Don't you have enough groupies following you around to pump up your ego? Do you really need to taunt me?"

"Yep, I do."

She laughed at his unexpected response. "Well, stop it."

Sighing, he took her hand. "I like you, Philly. And I like that you don't care which rodeo I've won or want to know which one I'm riding in next."

What Kate had confided earlier came to mind, and

curiosity almost got the better of Jessica. But she sensed that was a subject he wouldn't welcome her broaching. She liked the way he idly stroked her palm with the rough pad of his thumb, the touch so comfortable and casual as if they'd known each other a long time.

"See, I don't have to ask which rodeo you're riding in next. I already know you'll be riding tomorrow," she said teasingly, and wished she hadn't when his expression fell.

His thumb stopped the soothing circular motion. "Yeah, I guess I am."

"You don't sound terribly enthusiastic." She hoped he'd give her an opening.

He released her hand and grabbed his beer. "Can you keep a secret?"

"I promise not to tell anyone that you watch the food channel."

He smiled. "Can you keep two secrets?"

"Absolutely," she assured him, worried she'd sounded too flip when he looked so solemn.

"I'm sick of hearing about tomorrow's rodeo."

"That's your secret?" More than disappointed, she feared she'd put him off with her teasing.

"Around here, a statement like that comes right below saying you don't believe in God or that you hate football." He tipped the bottle to his lips and drained it.

"Seems to me you'd be excited about tomorrow," she prompted. "After all, you drove all night to get here."

"'Cause I owe these folks. Some of them travel hundreds of miles to Las Vegas or clear up to Montana or Fargo and then pay good money to watch me ride. This is my thank-you to them. I haven't missed a Fourth of July here in ten years."

"That's admirable," she said, "but I doubt anyone

expects you to break speed limits to get here, or force yourself to do something you don't want to do."

He smiled sadly, started to take another drink and then realized he'd finished the brew.

She took the empty bottle and set it aside, and then pressed her palms against his chest and forced him backward to a tall bar stool. "Sit. I'm tired of you towering over me."

"Pushy little thing, aren't you?"

"Yes, I can be," she said, "when it's important."

He chuckled. "It's important for me to sit?"

"Yes." She nodded seriously. "Please."

"Okay." He frowned, looking wary as he lowered himself to the stool.

"I'm sensing there's more to it about tomorrow." She took his big rough hands in hers. "Tell me."

He seemed startled, his expression growing guarded again. "You've been talking to Joe or Clint?"

"I don't even know them. I met them briefly at the graduation five years ago, but I haven't done more than wave at Clint since I've been here. As far as Joe, I don't think I'd even recognize him." Oh, she hoped he didn't push for more. Jessica didn't want to lie to him, although she really didn't know much. Only what she'd surmised from that off-the-cuff remark made by Kate.

He stayed studiously silent for a few seconds, and then moved her to the side while he shifted to a comfortable position on the stool and spread his legs. She thought the move was designed to put some distance between them, but then he drew her back, maneuvering her to stand between his thighs.

"Why, Philly?" He rejoined their hands and captured her gaze. "Why are you interested?"

The boldness of the forced intimacy unsettled her.

She was so close she could see the individual whiskers on his unshaven face. Would he kiss her again? Was he merely trying to distract her from the conversation?

"I like you," she said simply, and lifted a shoulder. "And it seems as though something is bothering you. I thought maybe you'd like to discuss it with someone who isn't emotionally invested in the community or the sport."

One side of his mouth lifted in a lopsided smile. "Pretty and smart. Maybe I should've gone to college."

She smiled back. "You're already pretty and smart."

He laughed and hugged her close. It was strictly a friendly hug, except that her body was inches from his groin and her nipples had sprung to life as soon as her breasts made contact with his chest. He buried his face in her hair, and she heard him inhale, felt the rise of his chest as his lungs filled. Even though she forced her hands to stay slack on his shoulders, and she tried her best not to think about how he'd looked without a stitch on earlier, the hug somehow changed from casual to sexual.

He suddenly smelled different, more musky and masculine, and his skin felt hot through the fabric of his shirt. Her own rising temperature had nothing to do with the late-afternoon sun, and if he didn't hurry up and kiss her, she would probably make the first move.

Slightly unsteady, she angled back to look at his face, to see if he was as affected as she was. His pupils were so large and dark, his eyes no longer looked blue. "You do realize we're on display in front of a thousand people," she whispered.

"I'd say only about seventy." His gaze stayed with hers as he stroked her cheek with his thumb.

"Oh, that's much better."

"You care?"

Oddly, she didn't, and shook her head.

"Good, because I'm going to kiss you."

She slid her arms around his neck, moving in closer, close enough to feel his arousal push against her lower belly. Dancing on the edge like this, here out in the open was incredibly foolish, she knew, and yet she really didn't care one iota. So very unlike her. Maybe it was because she didn't know anyone, except for Kate and the girls, of course.

If any of them saw her right now they'd be shocked. They'd wonder what had happened since college to make her so bold and reckless, to ignore the careful image she'd painstakingly cultivated. She hadn't been born with grace or money, not like her friends. She'd had to work hard for everything she'd ever achieved. Unfortunately, her ambition had left little room for intimacy.

Ben started on her lower lip, lightly touching it with the tip of his tongue. "Lucky for you there are kids around. I'll have to keep this G rated."

Stiffening, she reared her head back. The children. She'd totally forgotten. What was she doing?

"It's okay," he whispered hoarsely, keeping her in the circle of his arms. "I'm watching. They're all by the game booths and rides."

"Ben, no." She ducked away from his mouth.

"We're just kissing. No one can see how hard I am." His eyes were hooded, his lips damp and slightly parted, his plainspoken words evoking a primal response in her that defied understanding.

"I can't do this," she said, her eyes drifting closed, the temptation to succumb to his touch contradicting her words. "Not here."

"You feel so good."

"Oh, Ben, please, I'm not thinking straight." She hadn't planned on that disclosure, and embarrassment sobered her quickly. She lowered her arms to her sides and took a step back.

He shifted, trying subtly to adjust the front of his jeans. "I reckon you're right. This isn't the place. Hadn't figured on getting this carried away." He smiled wryly. "Your fault, you realize."

"Mine?" She did her own adjusting, straightening her collar and turning her sleeves back two more times in deference to the heat. Naturally, this did nothing for her internal temperature, which was totally out of control.

"You look too cute in those rolled-up jeans and over-size shirt."

She laughed. "Yeah, real sexy."

"Hmm." His lips twitching, his gaze ran down to the haphazard cuffs hiding all but the tips of her running shoes. "Don't get me revved up again."

"You are a royal pain in the butt." She planted her hands on her hips. "These—these duds weren't my idea, and I didn't have much choice at that."

"Just teasing you, Philly. Me, I'd like to see you in nothing."

She opened her mouth to admonish him, abruptly recalled this morning, him totally naked and gloriously male, and all other thoughts fled her mind.

His mouth curved in a knowing smile, almost as if he guessed what she'd been thinking. "You owe me."

"Only if your chili takes the blue ribbon."

They both sniffed the burned-smelling air at the same time, regarding each other with wide-eyed shock.

"Son of a bitch." Ben hopped off the stool and using

the bottom of his shirt, grabbed the handle and pulled the pot from the flame. "Damn it."

Jessica peered inside. The onions and garlic were scorched. The meat didn't look so good, either, but some of it that was sitting on top was salvageable. She pressed her lips together, trying not to laugh. He didn't look as if he were in the mood to find anything funny about this.

"Sorry about the language," he muttered, staring into the pot and shaking his head. "This is great. Just great."

"What happens now? Are you allowed to start over?"

"Beats me. Even so, now I'm low on ingredients."

"I have an extra onion," she offered. "No garlic, though."

He eyed her suspiciously. "Why would you want to help?"

She was already backing toward her station. "Because I don't want to hear any excuses when I beat the pants off you."

"Well, hell, darlin'," he said, pushing up his hat rim and giving her a suggestive wink. "If that was all you're aiming for, I could save you a lot of trouble."

6

THE WHOLE THING WAS A SHAM. An hour before the ribs and chicken that had been smoking all day were ready, the chili entries were judged. As Ben had predicted, he won. And Jessica now knew why he'd been so sure of himself.

The man's fan club knew no bounds. Seven women had judged, and anonymous or not, they quickly seemed quite certain which entry they wanted to award the blue ribbon, while they all made eyes at Ben. He probably could've burned the whole pot, it wouldn't have mattered. It was pretty laughable, really, except for the wasted time and effort of the other contestants. Why they even bothered entering was beyond Jessica's comprehension. But no one seemed to notice or care, and the sampling of all the different kinds of chili by everyone appeared to be the true highlight of the cook-off.

"Want to touch my ribbon?" he asked, coming up from behind her as she watched the new band set up on stage. He held two longneck bottles of beer in one hand and the first prize ribbon in the other.

She accepted the beer he offered and gave him a dry look. "How do they know which one is yours?"

"What do you mean?" He pretended confusion, but the frown wasn't quite genuine enough.

"How do the judges know?"

"Now, don't go being a sore loser." He tried to hide his smile as he chugged down some of the brew.

"All right. Don't tell me."

He chuckled. "Did it ever occur to you that I make a damn fine chili? Did you try it?"

"Did you try mine?" she countered.

"Actually, it was pretty good. Better than I expected, to tell you the truth."

She studied him, wondering if he was putting her on. "You tried it."

"Had a real kick to it I wasn't expecting."

She blinked. She had made it spicy the way she liked it. "I don't think you have any of yours left."

"I saved you a taste." His eyes gleamed with mischief, and she didn't miss his double meaning. "Come on."

He took her hand and led her through the crowd. They were stopped only twice, remarkable because it seemed as if he knew everyone. She spotted Dory near the grills with one of Kate's brothers, and it suddenly occurred to Jessica that she'd been here for over twenty-four hours and had spent nearly all of her time with Ben instead of her three friends.

Oddly, she didn't feel guilty. She could tell herself that it was because Dory looked happy to be with Clint, or that it was probably better to stay out of Kate's hair at this point. But she didn't even need the rationalizations, not when being with Ben was making her happier than she'd been in a long time.

She hadn't thought twice about her disheveled appearance or been concerned that every hair was in place. She wasn't worried about the importance of whom she met or how she was representing the magazine. In a crazy way she felt as if she were getting a second chance at the carefree college days she'd missed out on. Great, only twenty-seven and already living a second childhood.

"In here." Ben tugged her through the doorway of the shed where they'd picked up their supplies, and then closed the door.

"Oh, I see, you're going to show me your etchings."

"Hey, I don't need excuses to get you alone. I won the bet, remember?"

She lifted her chin. "You have absolutely no conscience if you insist on collecting."

He thought for a moment. "I can live with that."

She gave him her best schoolmarm head shake. "Why did you really bring me in here?"

He looked over at her, his brows arched in amusement, as if he knew that her pulse raced and her skin tingled just from being alone with him. "To give you this." He had tucked away a small foam cup covered with a white paper napkin. On it was a note that he quickly crumpled, but not before she saw that it read, "Ben Anderson's, paws off."

Smiling, she accepted the cup along with a plastic spoon, and tasted a small amount of the lukewarm chili. She took a second bite. It was really good. But she also noted how his entry was distinguished from everyone else's. He used both ground and cubed meat. Tricky devil.

"What do you think?" he asked proudly.

Jessica gazed up at him, realizing for the first time that this wasn't a big joke to him. "It's terrific."

"It's my grandmother's recipe," he said, shrugging. "I shouldn't take credit, although I did jazz it up a bit."

His sincerity blew her away. Big, tough, bronc-riding Ben looked like a little boy eager to please. She swallowed around the lump in her throat and sandwiched one of his hands between hers. "Take a bow, Mr. Anderson, you deserved to win."

Embarrassment flickered in his eyes, and then he grinned. "You're just saying that to get into my pants."

That startled a laugh out of her. "Damn, you saw right through me."

He brought one of her hands to his lips and pressed a kiss to the back. "This is going to sound weird, but I feel as though I've known you for a lifetime."

Her heart swelled. "It doesn't sound weird. I feel it, too."

He lowered his head and briefly touched his lips to hers. "Stay with me tonight," he whispered, and drew her lower lip between his teeth.

She closed her eyes when his warm, moist breath paved the way to the spot below her ear. A shiver of longing slipped down her spine, the yearning so great that it made her light-headed. Never in a million years would she have guessed that Ben was the kind of man who could make her feel this way. He was radically different from the professional, sophisticated men she met in Manhattan, or for that matter, the sort to which she was usually attracted.

Naturally she would spend the night with him. He needn't have asked. She was about to tell him so, when she heard someone outside yelling his name. At least she thought she had, and then Ben stiffened, and she knew the voice hadn't been her imagination.

"BEN ANDERSON, where you at, you sly son of a gun? Saw him just a minute ago. Anybody seen Ben? You in that shed, boy?"

Ben sighed with disgust when he recognized Harlan Samuels's loud tobacco-roughened voice just outside the shed. The man had to be pushing eighty by now, but that didn't give him the right to be out there howling like a coyote.

Jessica's eyes widened. "Do you know who that is?"

"Unfortunately." Ben scrubbed at his face, surprised to feel the extent of stubble covering his jaw. He had a nerve kissing Jessica the way he had without shaving. "I'd better go see what he wants, or he'll just annoy us until I do."

"Go, please."

He grinned and pulled her roughly against him. "Give me a kiss first. I'll try not to burn you with my whiskers."

"Where you at, Ben Anderson?" Harlan knocked on the shed's door. "You in there?"

Ben groaned. "Crazy old coot." He kissed the tip of her nose and then set her aside. "I'll get rid of him fast. Don't go away."

Before Ben could grab the doorknob, Harlan pushed open the door. Jessica shrank back into the corner, and Ben used his body to block the smaller man's view. She didn't strike him as shy over being caught alone in the shed with him, but he didn't want Harlan possibly making a crude joke at her expense.

"There you are, boy. I heard me a rumor that you better say ain't true." Harlan barreled his way in before Ben could meet him outside. The older man spotted Jessica, touched the brim of his Stetson and said, "How do, ma'am?" and then glared at Ben. "You want to talk in front of the lady?"

Ben rubbed the back of his neck. "What is it, Harlan?"

"Tell me you ain't quittin.' Let me hear it from your own mouth."

Ben stared, speechless, anger seeping in. How the

hell did— No way Clint or Joe would've said a word to anyone. "Where did you hear this?"

"Is it true, son?" Harlan's cloudy blue eyes pleaded with Ben to deny the rumor, his earlier bluster subsiding to a dull roar.

Ben inhaled deeply. He should've figured there wasn't a snowball's chance that he could keep a lid on the news until his announcement tomorrow. Not around these parts. "Look, Harlan, I want to keep this between us for right now," Ben said in a low voice, even while knowing that after the ruckus Harlan had just made it was going to be tough to keep their conversation quiet.

"So it's true," the old man murmured, the disappointment etched in his face making him look ten years older. "Thought I'd die before I'd see you quit. Good thing your granddad didn't live to see you do such a pitiful thing."

"It's not a matter of quitting. According to the doctors, I don't have a choice." Ben shot a glance at Jessica, who listened with avid interest. He'd almost told her about his impending retirement a couple of times. Mostly to get it off his chest, not because it would mean diddly-squat to her.

Harlan's weathered face softened. "I heard you took a nasty tumble in Abilene. Didn't know you were hurt that bad."

Not just Abilene, but San Antonio and Albuquerque and Dallas and the list went on. Ever since he'd broken his wrist a year ago, it had been getting harder and harder to keep going. When his leg had gotten stomped three months ago, he'd seen the writing on the wall. But it was the fracture at the top of his spine that was sidelining him. Either that or face possible paralysis the next time he was thrown.

"Look, Harlan, I don't know how you found out about my retirement, and I'm real sorry you didn't hear it from me first, your being granddad's best friend and all. The decision didn't come easy for me, and I only just made up my mind for sure after the San Antonio finals." He clamped a conciliatory hand on the old man's shoulder. "Hell, Harlan, I'm too old to be getting bucked around."

Harlan grunted. "Look at me, almost seventy and I still ride Thunder."

Ben snorted. "Almost what?"

"Hush now, boy," Harlan glanced over his shoulder and lowered his voice. "I been seeing the widow Perkins and she somehow got the idea I was a little younger than I am."

Ben chuckled. "Looks like we both have a secret to keep." He stopped and sobered. "Who else knows, Harlan?"

The man shrugged sheepishly. "I might've shot my mouth off a bit. But only because I thought it was a rumor and I was trying to get to the bottom of things. Sorry, son."

"It's all right." Ben swallowed back his annoyance. The man had meant no harm, and before Ben had even started making a living on the circuit, Harlan had been in his corner, rooting him on, telling everybody that someday Ben was going to be the best bronco rider in the country. "But do me a favor, tell me how you found out."

"It was Millie's boy, the widow Perkins's son," he clarified. "He works for Sundown in their headquarters in Dallas. Told me this morning that it looked like they were gonna start sponsoring that young Cody Meyers from Galveston. They don't generally sponsor two riders at the same time so I told him he had to be wrong, but he stuck to his guns. Started me to thinkin'."

Son of a bitch. Ben tried to remain calm when he really wanted to put his fist through the wall. After having sponsored him for the last eight years, the bastards hadn't said a word about dropping him. He'd made an appointment with them for next Wednesday, and granted, it was likely they'd already seen the writing on the wall, too. But to go behind his back…

"I won't say nothin' about our conversation to anyone," offered Harlan, sending a look of apology Jessica's way. "And if they ask, I'll tell 'em it's none of their dang business."

"Thanks, Harlan. I plan on making an announcement after the rodeo tomorrow."

Harlan had gotten to the doorway but frowned. "You up to riding? Maybe you ought to sit out tomorrow."

"I'm not an invalid," Ben grumbled, and then realized how churlish he'd sounded.

"Just don't be foolish, boy," Harlan said quietly. "Seems to me you had a good reason to come to that decision."

Ben watched him leave, loath to face Jessica. She was going to have questions, and the last thing he wanted to do was rehash the reasons he needed to stop doing the only thing in his life he'd been good at. And now he had his sponsor to think about. He'd wanted to be the one who told them it was over, that he wouldn't be renewing his contract with them, damn it. Show everyone he knew when it was time to bow out gracefully. But they'd already planned on getting rid of him.

"Hey." Jessica laid a hand on his shoulder.

Slowly he turned to face her. They'd only just met. He didn't owe her any answers.

"That barbecue is smelling way too good." The smile reached her eyes, mercifully hiding the questions he knew she had. "How about feeding me, cowboy? Then maybe I'll let you show me how to do that fancy two-step."

7

THE SMOKED CHICKEN and ribs that had smelled heavenly earlier tasted like cardboard. To be fair, the meat probably was perfection, but Jessica no longer had an appetite. Her heart ached for Ben.

He ate, smiled, even joked with some of the ranch hands with whom they shared a table during dinner, and although he'd kept quiet about the earlier discussion with Harlan, she knew he was hurting. When he thought no one noticed, his mind seemed to wander off, and when anyone brought up tomorrow's rodeo, the tic at the side of his neck went off like a jackhammer.

She couldn't imagine what he'd been going through. Retiring at his age was enough of a blow to the ego, especially since he was obviously at the top of his game, but giving up a corporate sponsorship, too? That had to mean turning his back on some serious endorsement money. Wow, was she ever getting a crash course in the rodeo business.

When no one was looking, she crumpled her paper napkin over her plate to hide the amount of food she couldn't force down and quickly disposed of the evidence in a nearby trash can. Most of the people had finished eating and had either moved to the dance floor or planted themselves in front of the band.

"Okay," she said when she returned to the table. "Are you going to show me how to dance?"

He'd just finished his last bite of corn bread. "I didn't figure you for the two-stepping type."

"Oh, you figured right. I'll totally trample your feet. I can't remember the last time I danced."

"You sure you want to do it now?"

No, she didn't, but if she could distract him she would. "Sure. Why not? I'm on vacation."

His lips tilted up slightly as if he knew exactly what she was trying to do. "Why not," he said, and got to his feet.

She took his hand, and he didn't object as she led him toward the dance floor. Perversely she noticed the envious looks from other women as they weaved around the rows of picnic tables. There were curious stares, too, from men and women alike, and a girl of about seven with long strawberry-blond hair even stopped them to ask if Jessica was his new girlfriend. Ben winked at the child, assured her she was still his number one girl and asked her to save him the next dance, which sent her into a giggling fit.

The song ended just as they stepped onto the dance floor. Jessica grinned, about to make a joke about the reprieve when Ben slid his arms around her waist, pulled her close and stared earnestly into her face. "You didn't even ask," he said, both curiosity and confusion in his eyes.

She knew exactly what he was talking about so didn't pretend otherwise. "If you want to, I'm sure you'll tell me."

"Thank you," he murmured, kissing her hair.

She tilted her head back to look at him, her chest tightening. With so many pairs of eyes focused on them, normally she'd feel self-conscious. But at this minute, nothing mattered but his strong arms holding her and the glint of admiration in his steady gaze.

It struck her how this was truly one of those movie moments, well orchestrated to swell the heart of every viewer. She would never have dreamed something like this could happen in real life, certainly not to her, and especially not with a man she'd known for only one day.

Not even the crowd swirling around them, or the loud whispers could break the spell. The band played a couple of notes of the next song, a slower moodier melody, and Ben splayed his hand across her lower back and took her hand.

A loud screech abruptly interrupted the music, startling Jessica. She and Ben jerked their gazes toward the stage, as did the other couples who'd moved close together for the slower number.

A short, rotund man grabbed the microphone. "Beg pardon for the interruption, folks," he said, "but I figured I'd best make this announcement while I got everyone's attention."

Ben muttered a mild curse, and then sighed heavily.

"What's wrong?" Jessica asked.

He shook his head, and stared grimly at the man whose gaze drew unerringly to Ben.

"I know I don't have to point out to all you good folks that tomorrow we'll have the honor of watching the country's best bareback rider in action." He grinned broadly. "I heard he drove all night to get here. What say we give Ben Anderson a round of applause?"

Everyone started clapping and whistling and stomping their feet. Ben's smile was obviously forced as he put up a silencing hand. The crowd responded by growing louder, until someone whistled into the microphone.

The annoying shrill did the trick, curbing the racket to a dull murmur.

Harlan had taken over the microphone. He waited until he had everyone's attention and then said, "This year, as grand marshal of the rodeo, I'm proposing we do something different. I say we give some of our young up-and-comers a chance at the title this year."

People exchanged looks, clearly confused, until one man hollered, "What are you saying, Harlan?"

"That it ain't fair if Ben rides. We all know he'll win and some of these young pups just starting out won't have a chance at—"

The crowd wouldn't let him finish. Some started booing, others laughed, thinking it was a joke. Harlan, his face flushed, looked helplessly at Ben.

"He's right." Ben quickly got everyone's attention. "You all have seen me ride. I hear we have some real talent right here at the Sugarloaf and over at the Double R. Maybe it's—"

"Hell, Ben, we know that, and they'll have their chance," a tall thin man with a droopy mustache cut in. "You know most of us can't be away from our ranches long enough to follow the circuit. This is the only time we get to see you ride except maybe on TV."

Jessica scanned the crowd, the heads nodding in agreement, the anxious expressions on faces that said the idea of Ben not riding was sheer blasphemy. More and more she understood what a big deal it was to have Ben here, how much his retirement would affect these people who worshipped their hometown hero.

"Harlan, you get any more harebrained ideas, keep 'em to yourself," an older grizzled cowboy said around a toothpick sticking out of his mouth. "Now let's hear some music."

"Wait a minute." Ben's voice rose above the chorus of people echoing their agreement. "Harlan was only trying to help because he knows something y'all don't." The crowd settled to a dull murmur. "No use me keeping quiet any longer, so I'm going to tell you straight out. After tomorrow, I'm done riding."

Stunned silence greeted his announcement. People stared back in shock, some of them exchanging looks of complete disbelief before returning their attention to Ben and gaping at him as if he'd just denounced their beloved state.

"Why?" The inevitable question came from somewhere deep in the crowd.

"Every rider knows when it's time to get out of the saddle, whether it's because he's too old or too beat-up." Ben rubbed the back of his neck, looking as if he wanted to be anywhere on earth besides standing here in front of all these disappointed people. "I was going to wait and tell y'all tomorrow, but I—" He shrugged. "No point to it."

A few people moved forward with concern in their eyes. "Heard you got banged up pretty good in Abilene," said a tall middle-aged man with bushy sideburns. "Got your arm hurt."

Ben laughed wryly. "Yeah." He gingerly touched his wrist, and then reached for Jessica. "If you folks will excuse me, I promised this lady a dance."

She went gladly into his arms. The band took it as their cue to resume playing and picked up where they'd left off with a slow country song. The floor remained sparing of couples as people continued to talk amongst themselves, their gazes never straying far from Ben.

"I know that was hard for you," she whispered.

He shrugged indifferently, his heart beating hard and fast against her breast.

"Don't play the tough guy with me. It won't work."

He drew back to look down at her, the corners of his mouth twitching. "I am tough. And macho. And—"

"And full of you know what."

Smiling, he hugged her tightly against him, and rested his chin on top of her head. "I can't believe I've finally said it out loud," he murmured. "I must've spent three hours rehearsing what I was going to say."

"Working up to the deed is always the worst part."

"Not exactly," he said quietly.

She bit her lip. There was so much she wanted to say but would her opinions and questions be welcome? Dare she risk alienating him? She'd invited his confidence earlier, but he'd remained circumspect. That was enough to tell her to keep her mouth shut. Still, she didn't want to appear unsympathetic, nor disinterested. Selfishly she hated that the mood had changed, that an hour ago she'd fully expected to end up in his bed, but now, she wasn't so sure.

She silently cleared her throat. "So what are your plans?"

"To get through that ride tomorrow in one piece."

Jessica jerked back to look at him. "Are you serious?"

"Darlin', that is always the number one goal." He frowned, his expression one of instant regret, as if he'd said too much. "Don't look at me like that. I was just teasing."

But she knew he wasn't. A sickening thought registered. "Were you ordered by a doctor not to ride anymore?"

His jaw tightened. "I'll be fine. I've already seen the bronc they have for me. Piece of cake."

"Don't do it, Ben."

"Come on now." His anxious gaze shifted to the couple dancing close enough to hear them. "A final ride isn't going to kill me," he said close to her ear.

Dread clogged her throat and then slid down to coil inside her belly. She sincerely hoped he was right.

THE MINUTE AFTER he'd opened his mouth, Ben knew it had been a mistake to make the announcement tonight. And he wouldn't have done it except he couldn't stand to see everyone making fun of Harlan. On the one hand Ben was glad it was over with, but then, too, he felt responsible for the sudden subdued tone of the crowd. July Fourth here at the Sugarloaf was an event everyone looked forward to every year. He hadn't wanted to ruin everything. Did they think he *wanted* to retire? He was only thirty-two, and one of the top prizewinners on the circuit.

Luckily he'd invested well and money wouldn't be a problem for some time. In fact, he'd had his eye on a spread south of the panhandle he could pay cash for and still have enough left to buy some fine animals. A stockman's life wouldn't be as exciting as the one he'd led for the past fourteen years, but maybe it was time to settle down. Sleep in the same bed every night. No, he didn't want anyone's pity, and he wasn't about to cry the blues because life had been one hell of a good ride so far. But he could use some understanding.

Jessica had gotten pretty tense, too, and he had no idea what to do about it. He wasn't even sure what her problem was, other than she was needlessly worried for him. But hell, they'd just met this morning. She'd get over it.

They both stayed silent for the remainder of the song, her spine as rigid as a branding iron. He tried in vain to think of something to say, anything that might reclaim some of their earlier playfulness. He had a feeling he was going to be sleeping alone tonight.

"Hey, Ben, you up for some poker with the boys later?" Jake, a Double R cowhand, asked before the band slid into their next number.

He met Jessica's noncommittal gaze. Maybe that's just what he needed to take his mind off tomorrow. Off Jessica. "Sure. Tell me where and when."

8

THE NEXT MORNING, for the first time since Jessica could remember, she skipped her run. Even in snow she ran. It didn't matter that she often worked thirteen-hour days, she always made time to exercise. It wasn't the physical release she craved as much as the illusion of control over her crazy life.

Ironically, this morning she needed the run more than ever yet couldn't seem to make herself do it. She not only felt out of control, but totally out of her element. She'd slept poorly, thinking about Ben sleeping only two doors down, or maybe he hadn't slept at all but rather stayed up all night, drinking and playing poker. The jerk.

That wasn't fair. He was free to do as he pleased. As it was, she'd monopolized most of his day. But still, she couldn't believe last night had ended the way it had. Her in her room, alone, staring at the shadows on the ceiling, replaying events of the day in her head.

She quickly showered and dressed, knowing that with the barbecue over, Kate would be free to enjoy the day. Although knowing Kate, she was probably busy cooking breakfast. Jessica followed the aroma of cinnamon, hoping it wasn't too late to have some private time with her friend, and sure enough, found Kate at the stove, frying bacon.

"Do you sleep in the kitchen, too?" Jessica headed

for the coffeepot, winking at Maria, who was cutting up a melon.

Kate grinned over her shoulder. "This is it for me. I'm turning the kitchen back over to Maria, and I'm not touching another pot or pan for a month." She made a face. "I'm sorry I've been so inattentive. It usually isn't crazy like this."

Passing by the cinnamon buns cooling on racks, Jessica sniffed appreciatively. "Can I help?"

"Nope." Kate grabbed a mug off the counter, refilled it with coffee and motioned for Jessica to join her at the table. "I don't think Dory or Lisa are up yet. I'm surprised you are."

Jessica wondered if that was in reference to Ben. "I hope we're going to finally meet your fiance today."

Frustration flashed in Kate's eyes, and she took a quick sip of coffee before producing a strained smile. "I hope so, too. Everyone brings their own picnic dinners to eat after the rodeo and while we watch fireworks. He promised to be here."

The rodeo. God, just the word sent dread slithering down her spine. "I wish he wouldn't ride," Jessica said miserably, all pretense out the window.

Kate nodded, looking just as glum. "I'm glad you brought it up. I can't go into detail without betraying a confidence, but he can't ride, Jessica. It's too risky."

"You have to stop him." Jessica's stomach lurched. "Did your brothers talk to him? Can't they make him see reason?"

"They tried, but…I know I shouldn't ask this, but I thought maybe you could try."

"Me? He barely knows me."

Kate smiled gently. "I saw the two of you yesterday, and I know Ben. He's practically a brother to me, too.

Trust me when I tell you that you just might have an impact."

Jessica wrapped both hands around her mug and brought it to her lips, her thoughts spiraling wildly. What did she have to lose? He'd probably rightfully tell her it was none of her business. So what? If there was a chance… "Where is he?"

Kate shrugged. "I was hoping he'd been with you."

Smiling wickedly, Jessica glanced at the clock. Three hours until the rodeo started. "I think I know what to do."

BEN SILENTLY CURSED himself for staying up so late with the boys. Good thing he'd gone light on the beer and skipped the tequila shots or he'd really be hurting. It had been tempting, though, to climb into a bottle and lose himself for a while. Not only had he regretted not spending the night with Jessica, but he didn't want to ride today. Funny, because he thought he'd be depressed knowing it was likely to be his last ride.

After toweling off from his shower, he pulled on a pair of boxers and jeans, his gaze on the bedside clock. Hell, almost noon already. The rodeo started in an hour, although he couldn't recall when he was scheduled to ride. His thoughts strayed to Jessica just as a knock sounded at the door. Probably Clint wanting to tell him again what a dumb ass he was.

He hunkered down to see if he'd kicked his boots under the bed last night, and saw the ones he'd bought for Jessica, still in the box. "Come in."

The door opened and it was her, wearing an oversize white robe. Barefoot, she padded in and closed the door behind her. "I was worried I hadn't caught you in time."

"I just got out of the shower." He found his boots and got to his feet. "Did you just get up?"

Shaking her head, she tightened the sash around her waist. She looked nervous at first, but then her gaze ran down his chest to the waistband of his jeans, and longing flared in her eyes. The blatancy of it caught him off guard, and his entire body reacted. Trying not to be obvious, he sat at the edge of the bed, shifting against the snugness of his fly and wondering what was under that robe. He saw only skin at the V.

"Last night, I…" She moistened her lips. "I missed you."

He had a sinking feeling he knew where this was going. "Yeah, well…" He cleared his throat. "I was stupid."

She smiled. And then let one side of the robe slip down her shoulder. Her bare shoulder. "It occurred to me that you never collected on your bet. And…" She let the other side slip off, barely holding the fabric together over her breasts. "It seems unfair that I got to see yours but you didn't see mine."

Damn her. He couldn't seem to look away, waiting to see what she exposed next. "You picked a fine time, Philly." Frustrated, he sighed. "I know what you're doing."

Jessica untied her sash. "Oh, did I mention—" she let the robe drop to the floor "—this is a one-time offer."

Ben's heart slammed against his chest. She was perfect. High plump breasts, small pink nipples, tightly budded, a flat belly and a narrow waist with curvy hips. His gaze fastened to the juncture of her thighs and his cock immediately thickened. Man. He'd heard of a Brazilian wax but obviously hadn't understood the full concept until now.

"Damn you, Jessica, you're playing dirty."

She moved closer, coyly touching one of her nipples. "You think so?"

Groaning, he snaked an arm around her waist,

sliding his hand over her smooth, firm rear end and roughly bringing her toward him. With her breasts level with his face, he drew a nipple into his mouth, rolling his tongue over the sweet ripeness. She arched her back and fisted his hair, telling him this was exactly what she wanted.

He tasted the other nipple, while using both hands to cup her bottom, stretching and reaching his fingers between her thighs to feel her wetness. She was smooth and slick and he wanted desperately to lay her on her back, spread her legs and run his tongue over all that enticing silkiness.

She reached between them and unsnapped his jeans, the movement bunching her breasts together so that he could drawn both nipples into his mouth. He suckled greedily, amazed at his lack of restraint. He hadn't been this uncontrollably horny since he was seventeen years old. Obsessing over the Brazilian wax was the problem.

With gentle force he urged her away from him, and then stood and stripped off his jeans and boxers. He kissed her and started to lay her down on the bed, when he flashed on the time. The rodeo. This was crazy. He couldn't just blow everyone off.

JESSICA SENSED his mood shift, saw his gaze draw to the bedside clock. "Please, don't. You know it's foolish."

"I owe these people," he said, softly stroking her cheek.

"If they really care about you, they won't want you to take the risk."

"They don't understand."

"Make them." She wrapped her hand around his hard swollen cock, at the base, and slowly pumped upward. Of course she wasn't playing fair. She didn't care. "Be totally honest."

He closed his eyes and groaned, moving against her palm. "You're an evil little witch," he whispered. "Know that?"

"I do." It took no effort to get him to lie back against the pillows, and then she crawled in alongside him.

She gave his penis a teasing lick, flattening her tongue over the silky moist crown, before gliding up his chest, her distended nipples grazing his skin. He caught her mouth with his and kissed her deeply, his tongue pushing for entrance she readily permitted. He moved his hand along the side of her hip and then stroked her bottom. She instinctively curled toward him, but he startled her by drawing away.

Breaking the kiss, he locked gazes with her, his eyes glazed. "I want to look at you," he said huskily.

She didn't understand at first, but he showed her by moving back farther and running his palm from her chest over her belly to the juncture of her thighs. His gaze followed the path of his hand and then he urged her legs apart. The appreciation in his eyes made her burn so hot inside she thought she might explode without him touching her. But then he spread her nether lips, his fingers barely glimpsing that oh-so-sensitive nub and to her utter astonishment, it was enough. The spasms started.

When she cried out, quickly biting down on a knuckle to subdue the sound, he looked as shocked as she was. Then he smiled, slid down and let his tongue take over, laving and circling and driving her to the edge of insanity, until her orgasm grew so intense she thought she'd die from it.

She finally had to push him away or risk shattering into a thousand fragile pieces. His reluctance to stop turned her on all over again. "I hope you have a condom," she whispered, annoyed at how foolish she'd been to come unprepared.

He got up to get one out of his jeans' pocket, and she couldn't help but stare, not sure if she should be impressed or intimidated by his striking hard-on. He quickly sheathed himself and too late, she realized she should be drawing this out until the rodeo started. But her need for him went far beyond providing a distraction. She wanted him inside her, wanted him to fill her with his heat.

Ben wasted no time in positioning himself between her thighs, but he didn't enter her right away. He lightly trailed his fingers over the puffy flesh that had been waxed smooth. "I like it," he murmured hoarsely. "This Brazilian wax business."

Impatient, she lifted her shoulders off the bed to reach the tip of his cock and used her palm in a circular motion. He tensed, briefly closing his eyes before shoving her hand aside and thrusting forward until his penis nudged her opening. There he stilled, using his fingers to test her wetness before slowly sliding inside, his glassy gaze fastened on the act.

She moved her hips, and he grasped her bent knees and sank deeper inside, a low husky moan escaping his lips. His chest heaved, his head went back and with increasing momentum he drove into her over and over again. She bucked up to meet each thrust, her entire body trembling until the spasms claimed her again.

He continued to pump into her, his cock rubbing her oversensitive clit. She squeezed her inner muscles, wanting his climax to be every bit as powerful. From the way his body tensed, his moan primal, it was.

Finally, he flopped onto his back and took her with him. Cradling her to his chest, he gently kissed her forehead. She melted against him, trying to catch her breath. His body was damp and warm, and so was hers. She hadn't even recovered and her thoughts went straight to the rodeo. He still had time….

"Ben?" She lifted her head to meet his eyes. "Please—"

"Shh." He stroked her hair. "Let's not ruin things."

Gazing into his beautiful blue eyes and thinking that anything bad could happen to him, she felt a sharp tug at her heart. Just because they'd had sex didn't give her any special rights, but she couldn't let it go. "See, the thing is, I know you don't want to ride. If you did, it would be different."

"Who says I don't?"

"Do you?"

He briefly closed his eyes. "You don't understand."

"What happens if you get hurt?"

"Hell, Jessica." He tried to pull away, but she wouldn't let him. Instead, he sighed and stared at the ceiling.

She let him have his silence for a few minutes and then said, "It's hard to just drop something you're good at. Until I had this job at the magazine, I was always the outsider, the scholarship kid who had to work twice as hard as everyone else to feel like I belonged."

He slid her a glance. "Here I thought you were from one of those rich families from back East."

"Not even close. I worked my butt off through school. I still do," she said quietly. "Because I'm terrified that if I so much as blink it will all slip away." The frank admission unsettled her. Not a subject she usually dwelled on. She smiled wryly. "How many times have I read in my own magazine that we should never let what we do define who we are?"

"Okay, Philly, I get your point."

"Do you?" She had a lot to sort out for herself, but for him right now, there was too much at stake. "Be honest, and ask yourself if one more ride is worth the risk. I promise not to say any more."

An excruciating amount of silence lapsed before he spoke. "I guess they've all seen me ride enough over the years."

"Oh, Ben." She hugged him tightly, surprised at the threatening sting of tears behind her eyes.

"About our bet."

"Yes?" she said cautiously.

"What are you doing in two weeks?"

The question was so surprising, it took a moment for her to adjust. In two weeks, she'd be completely insane with the anniversary issue. "Why?"

He smiled and idly rubbed her nipple. "What's halfway between New York and Houston? Nashville, huh?"

"I think so." Her insides started to quake, the quivery feeling quickly traveling to her arms and legs.

"Wait a second." He released her and rolled over to the edge of the bed, giving her a great view of his broad muscled back. He leaned over, reaching under the bed, and then sat up with a large shoe box in his hand. With a sheepish grin, and looking adorably uncertain, he handed her the box.

She opened it, and stared at the boots in disbelief.

"You don't have to keep them if you don't want to," he muttered. "It won't hurt my feelings or anything."

She swallowed back the lump in her throat, wondering if she should admit that he was the first man to have surprised her with a gift. She wanted to meet him in two weeks. She did, but with her crazy deadlines she couldn't possibly afford more time off. Which made her wonder why her lips curved into a smile. And why, before she leaned close to capture a kiss, she told him, "They'll be perfect for Nashville."

WILDFIRE

1

GOOD THING LISA STEVENS had always been willing to do anything to get a story. Even ride a willful horse under the blistering July sun in the middle of nowhere, to find a man who apparently didn't want to be found. Still, it had been a while since she'd climbed onto a saddle. Three years ago to be exact. She'd followed a lead to Nogales, Mexico, and spent two days in the desert with a grumpy drunk guide and an animal that was more mule than horse.

"Come on, Selma," she cooed to the stubborn bay mare, while pulling on the reins. "Slow down, girl."

The Sugarloaf Ranch foreman had sworn Selma was the gentlest mare in the stable. Yeah, right. Joe Manning had probably anticipated her looking for him and ordered the man to make sure she was given the most difficult animal of the lot. If she ended up on her rear in the dirt, she was going to wring his neck. Oh, hell, she'd planned on wringing his neck, anyway. He'd snubbed her for a day and a half now, and she was sick of it.

"Selma, I've had it with you." Lisa jerked the reins, half expecting to go flying over the mare's head.

To her relief, the horse slowed, and then stopped abruptly to graze on a grassy knoll. Lisa slowly released a breath, and in that instant recognized how tense she'd been for the twenty-minute ride. Unfortunately, she still had another twenty-minute return trip to the ranch. And only if she turned around now and gave up on looking for Joe. Damn him. What a coward.

She shaded her eyes against the late-afternoon sun and scanned the area where she'd been told he was mending fences. Lots of mesquite and scraggly yuccas broke up the acres and acres of green pastureland, but little else. She didn't even see any cows. Or for that matter, the line shack Kate said that he worked out of near where the path forked.

Swiping at the hair that clung to her damp cheek, Lisa twisted in the saddle to make sure she hadn't imagined the landmark fork. The dirt road sort of meandered to the left more than actually split. In fact, it wasn't much of a road, although she could see tire tracks from a small pickup or Jeep. But no line shack. Maybe she was in the wrong place.

If she had any sense, she'd turn around and go back to the ranch. The Fourth of July festivities hosted by her friend Kate's family was in full swing. Their neighbors for miles were there at the Sugarloaf, eating barbecue and getting ready for the dance. Kate and Lisa's other two college roommates were there, too. Dory had flown in from Hawaii and Jessica from New York for the reunion, not because they cared about the annual celebration but because Kate had announced her engagement.

And what was Lisa doing, instead of spending her time with them? Looking for Kate's brother Joe. Although it had been Kate's suggestion. Lisa wondered if her friend knew about graduation night, how Lisa had practically thrown herself at Joe, and he'd called her a foolish child.

Maybe at twenty-two she still had been a kid.

Spoiled certainly, by wealthy, doting, older parents who'd almost given up on having a child until Lisa had come along. But she wasn't a kid now. For the past five years she'd worked hard to prove she was a good reporter. Never turned her nose up at even the most trivial story. Got down and rolled around in the dirt when she had to. Her family name may have opened a door for her at the prestigious Chicago newspaper, but she'd proved her worth.

She lifted the hair from the back of her clammy neck, annoyed that the only purpose the ride had served was to require her to take another shower. Maybe he'd still show up at the barbecue since he'd promised Kate. The dance was probably out of the question but Lisa would find a way to get him alone at some point. Not only did she have a thing or two to tell him, she wanted another look. Wanted to know if he was as hot as she remembered. Silly really, because so what if he was. He'd made it plain that he wasn't interested in her. Which was probably half of his appeal. Joe Manning was the only man who'd ever turned her down.

After taking a final look toward a cluster of mesquite trees that could obscure a shack, she tightened the reins, hoping she could get Selma to turn around without a struggle. Whispering words of encouragement, she directed the mare to face east, toward the ranch.

Something blue near an outcropping of rocks caught her eye. She squinted and saw him then, standing beside the stream, watching her. He was too far away for her to make out his expression, but she could easily imagine that sardonic lift of one dark brow, his lips pulled into a thin, disapproving line. Of course there was a chance that wasn't even him, but she doubted it. Instinct told her it was Joe, who hadn't had the decency to flag her down.

Digging her heels into the horse's flank, she urged Selma toward him, and as they got closer she saw that his horse, obscured by some oak brush, was drinking from the stream. Immediately he turned away from her to hunker down and dip a red bandanna into the water. After using it to mop his face, he slowly rose, looking taller and leaner than she remembered. He hooked his thumbs into the waistband of his jeans and watched as she approached.

She recognized him, all right. The broad shoulders, the confident tilt of his strong square jaw, the short wavy black hair that hadn't changed in five years. "Joe?" she asked just to be difficult. "Joe Manning?"

"Who's asking?"

Lisa smiled, knowing she deserved that response. Selma seemed interested in having a drink and moved faster toward the stream. Lisa gave the mare her head and spent her energy checking out Joe. She'd caught a glimpse of him once yesterday, only briefly, from afar. Up close was so much better. He had a great mouth with a lush lower lip and a rugged yet freshly shaven face. In fact, he looked so clean-cut he could've been military issue.

The unwavering, midnight-blue eyes, so dark they hardly seemed blue was what got to her the most. Impossible to guess the man's thoughts. She'd never met anyone with that good a poker face, and that said a lot, since in her line of work her contacts ran the gamut from drug dealers to practiced politicians.

"Lisa Stevens," she said when Selma stopped a few feet away. "We've met before."

The brow went up, but not even a flicker of recognition crossed his face. Yup, he was good. Except she knew better. Thanks to Kate.

"I'm Kate's college friend. You came for the graduation ceremony." She waited for him to at least blink, or cry uncle. "Surely you remember. I tried to seduce you."

That got his attention. Both eyebrows went up, and the barest hint of a smile tugged at one side of his mouth. "Right," he said, his wry tone indicating he remembered enough.

She swung down from the saddle, enormously pleased with herself. "Although as you'd so plainly put it, I was just a child then." She glanced around for something to which she could tether the reins.

"I'll take that." He reached out, his tanned forearm corded with muscle. His hands were large and callused, with two long, thin scars streaking up from his wrist.

"Thank you." She purposely brushed his palm with her fingernails as she turned over the reins. She didn't know why. Just to see if she'd get a reaction, she supposed. Although what did a casual touch mean?

"What are you doing out here?" he asked while tying the mare to a branch near where his roan gelding drank from the stream.

"Looking for you."

"Why?" He seemed genuinely annoyed, which put a sizable dent in her ego.

"There's a party going on at your place. I'm sure you've noticed."

Unfazed by her sarcasm, he crouched down to dip his bandanna in the water again. "Did everything come to a screeching halt because I wasn't there?"

"You're the host. You're supposed to be there."

"Host?" He snorted. "This isn't Chicago."

He'd remembered where she was from? She smiled triumphantly at his slip of the tongue. But since he

didn't notice, she decided not to point out his faux pas.
She'd save that tidbit for later in case he really got on
her nerves.

As he straightened, he squeezed out some of the
water and then used the bandanna to pat the back of his
neck. The top two buttons of the Western-cut chambray
shirt he wore were unfastened, and she could see a
sprinkling of dark hair. Not too much, just enough to
draw her eye. Enough to make her wonder about the
rest of his chest.

"It's still hot for being nearly five." She forced her
gaze away and studied the stream, so shallow that she
suspected it might be seasonal.

"This is Texas, sweetheart, and it's summer. Yeah,
it's hot. Why don't you go back to the party and get
yourself a cold glass of lemonade."

"You wouldn't be trying to get rid of me, would
you?"

Joe opened his mouth to say something, but then
gave a small shake of his head and pressed the
bandanna to his throat.

Lisa smiled. "Come back with me. They'd just
started to serve the chicken and ribs when I left."

"I'll be there."

"When?"

"Later."

She sighed. "Kate won't be happy."

"My sister knows a ranch can't run itself."

Lisa got down on one knee, cupped some water in
her hands and splashed her face. It was warmer than
she'd expected and not nearly as refreshing as she'd
hoped. Still, it was wet and that counted for a lot right
now. She gathered her hair and pulled it over her left
shoulder, loosened her collar and then followed his

lead, using her hand to dampen the back of her neck. The effort helped marginally.

She looked up at him and found him studying her with a wariness that startled her. Did he think she was going to strip right here? "You wouldn't happen to have another one of those bandannas, would you?"

He frowned, checked his back pocket and shook his head. "It won't get cooler for another hour, so I'd head back to the ranch now if I were you."

"Can't do that." She bent to take a sip and stopped. "Is this water drinkable?"

"The horses seem to think so."

"Come on, seriously."

"It's still flowing pretty well. I filled my canteen here earlier. What do you mean you can't do that?"

She sipped a little, not sure she trusted him. The water did taste good, though. "I feel responsible, and I'm not going back without you."

"Responsible? What the blazes are you talking about?"

"You've been avoiding me, Joe." She shrugged. "Admit it. And in doing so, you're ignoring everyone else."

His face was full of expression now. Darker than a wintry Chicago night. "Next time you come out in the sun, wear a hat." He pointed to his own head, indicating that he thought she was nuts.

"I understand why you've been avoiding me. I do. Maybe if we talk about that night it won't be so awkward between us, and you'll feel free to join the party."

His narrowed gaze conveyed his distaste for that idea. "Did it ever occur to you that I haven't given that night another thought?"

"I'm sure you haven't, at least not until Kate invited

me here." Lisa wished she could say the same. His rejection had stung for days, but the real kicker had been knowing she'd made an utter fool of herself. She'd been tipsy from too much celebratory champagne, pouty and petulant, and suddenly thinking about it made her cringe even after all these years.

Funny how she'd successfully blocked out most of the specifics until now. She really had been pretty awful. Not ready to look at him, she splashed more water on her face, felt the drops trickle down her throat. The memory robbed her of the excitement of seeing him again. Too late, it occurred to her that she should have let it go, pretended the incident had never happened.

She cautiously rose, aware that all her splashing had made some of the rocks around her feet slick. When she was confident she wouldn't slip, she straightened fully. "Look, I'm asking you to forgive me for being a foolish kid back then." She smiled, and noticed that his gaze had flickered twice to the front of her shirt. "You were the tall, dark, handsome older man," she said with a teasing note in her voice. "All the girls wanted to—"

In answer, he turned and headed for the hat he'd left on a rock, his boots crunching hard and determined on the rocky ground. "Go back to the party, Lisa," he called over his shoulder.

"Joe, wait. I'm not sure I know the way back."

After grabbing the hat, he set it on his head, then jerked the reins of his horse free of the branch, and swung into the saddle. He rode off in the opposite direction of the ranch, without looking back.

2

JOE CLENCHED HIS TEETH so hard he was gonna end up giving himself a headache. Had she gotten the front of her shirt wet on purpose? He could tell she'd been wearing a bra, but it sure wasn't much of one. Right through her pink cotton shirt he could see the darkened outline of her hardened nipples. That woman was nothing but trouble. Had been from the first minute he'd met her back East at that fancy college his sister had attended. Clearly Lisa hadn't changed. She was irritating and pushy, and she sure as hell didn't know when to keep her mouth shut. She was also the most beautiful woman he'd ever met.

Thinking about all that long, pale blond hair, those inquisitive blue eyes and her creamy skin had screwed up his sleep for a good week after he'd returned to Texas. She'd been flirty and playful from the moment Kate had introduced them, and with three flutes of champagne in her belly at the postgraduation reception, she'd made it real plain that he'd be welcome in her bed. The sweet, unexpected kiss she'd pressed to his mouth ironically had knocked some sense into him.

Even though it had taken every ounce of gumption he possessed, he'd politely backed off, and like a whipped pup with his tail between his legs, he took a cab to his hotel room and ordered up a bottle of scotch.

She was young and his baby sister's friend. No way he would've taken advantage of the impulsive invitation she'd extended.

All and all the offer had been harmless, no reason for him to give it another thought, but what he found unforgivable was that she'd made him feel old and worn-out, as if he didn't have the right to forget his burdens for even one night. Sadly, he'd been only twenty-eight at the time.

His reaction hadn't been her fault. The blame belonged to no one but himself. His parents' premature death had forced him to accept responsibilities for which he hadn't been prepared. After the initial shock had worn off, he'd resented dropping out after his sophomore year of college to run the ranch. But since Clint and Kate had both been too young to handle the operation, Joe had no choice.

Now, older and wiser, he regretted none of it. He was proud of what the ranch had become under his leadership, prouder still of Clint's and Kate's academic accomplishments and that he'd been able to provide them the opportunity to attend top-notch schools. Given the choice, he'd do it all over again. He just didn't need someone like Lisa popping up and reminding him of old crap.

Lisa Stevens.

Hell, he'd finally gotten her name out of his head, and then Kate had informed him that she'd invited her college roommates for the long weekend. He'd gotten an earful then about what a hotshot reporter Lisa was in Chicago, about how she traveled all over the country covering important stories and how last year she was the youngest person to win a coveted prize for journalism. Apparently she was a shoe-in for another award this year. So she'd done well. Good for her. She should be smart enough to figure out that he wanted to be left alone.

After riding for over five minutes, he realized he was headed away from the fence that he'd intended on mending. He muttered a curse and drew his horse in a wide circle so that he could see toward the stream and make sure she hadn't followed before he headed back that way.

He didn't believe for one second that she didn't know how to get back to the ranch. That claim had been manipulation, pure and simple. She was probably well on her way back, her full, tempting lips pursed in a perfect pout, and sure as the sun would set, there would be a line of guys waiting to ask her for the first dance.

Although he'd originally planned on catching the tail end of the barbecue, then making a brief appearance at the dance, now he wasn't sure. Being near her seemed to cloud his good sense. But she was right, he didn't want to be antisocial on her account. During this busy time of year, he didn't see most of his neighbors for long stretches. This was a big weekend for everyone in the community, game booths and rides for the kids, the chili cook-off, the barbecue and dance, tomorrow the rodeo and fireworks. It was a time they all relaxed and caught up on what was going on with each other.

He decided to finish the last stretch of fence, grab a shower, chow down on some ribs and chicken and Maria's corn bread, maybe indulge in a beer or two. He'd still hit the sack early. Tomorrow he had two irrigation pipes to fix before the rodeo started. Lisa wouldn't be bothering him. Too many men to vie for her attention. By the time he returned to the ranch, she'd be knee-deep in the damn fools.

Not two minutes later he saw her. Still by the stream,

right where he'd left her, the hem of her shirt pulled from her waistband and tied up high under her breasts.

"I WAS HOPING you'd come back this way." She smiled up at him, wishing his eyes weren't shaded by his hat.

He didn't return the smile. In fact, he seemed annoyed. But at least he'd stopped and hadn't galloped past her. "Why are you still here?"

"Enjoying the fresh air."

"There's plenty of that at the ranch." He flicked the reins and the beautiful animal lifted his powerful front hoof.

"Wait."

Joe hesitated, but she could tell by his defensive posture that he was tempted to ignore her and keep going.

She grabbed her shoes and socks that she'd removed in order to wade into the stream and picked her way over to where he stayed mounted on his horse.

"You don't want to walk around barefooted like that," he said, his lips pulled thin, giving him the appearance of a disapproving father.

"If I'd stopped to put on my shoes I was afraid you'd leave. Ouch." Something prickly latched on to the tender skin of her arch. She quickly brought her foot up to investigate, but the heel of her other foot met the same fate. "Holy crap." She removed the small burr from her arch but was afraid to put her rescued foot down. If she could just get her shoe on first…

With a loud sigh of disgust, he climbed off his horse and walked toward her. "Here."

Miffed that he seemed so put out, she placed a balancing hand on the arm he offered, tempted to remind him that she hadn't asked for his help. But the enticing feel of corded muscle beneath her palm made her forget everything else. Made her want to feel more of him. The man had to be as strong as the proverbial ox.

While trying to pull her sock on, she stepped down too hard on her affected heel. "Ouch. Ouch. Ouch."

"Ah, hell." He grabbed her by the waist, surprising a whoop out of her, and lifted her onto his horse, side-saddle so that her legs dangled off the gelding's ribs. "Stay, Rebel," he ordered the animal.

She clutched the saddle horn with both hands, expecting the gelding to start bucking with all the commotion, but Rebel was obviously well trained and did nothing more than whinny. Still, she wasn't about to let both hands go, so how did he expect her to get her shoes and socks on?

Joe soothingly patted the horse's flank and then after a brief hesitation, he easily manacled her ankle with his large hand and long, lean fingers where she'd rolled up the cuffs of her jeans.

Pedicure last week. Shaved this morning. The panicky checklist flew through her head as he lifted her foot to examine the underneath. Even her size-eight foot looked small against his large palm. He found the burr and plucked it from her heel, and then ran the tip of his finger along her arch.

She jerked her leg and stifled a giggle. "I'm ticklish," she admitted when he stared up at her with those serious blue eyes.

He said nothing, the old sourpuss, just bent his head again and inspected her sole.

"I think there was only that one." She relaxed her hold when her hand started to cramp.

"Give me your socks."

She'd forgotten she still had them squashed between her palm and the saddle horn. She clutched them tighter, abhorring the thought of him handling her already-worn socks, and then sliding them on as if she were a child. "I think I can do it."

He tilted his head back, adjusted the rim of his hat and almost smiled. "Be my guest," he said, and stepped back, folding his muscled arms across his chest.

Tentatively, she released the saddle horn and bent slightly at the waist. At the movement, the horse stepped high, jostling her. She made a grab for the saddle horn again, missing it the first time, and nearly ended up sliding off backward. Joe hadn't so much as flexed a muscle. Would he have tried to catch her if she fell?

The horse stomped impatiently.

Lisa hung on for dear life. "Tell him not to do that."

"Rebel, don't do that," Joe said sternly, amusement glinting in his eyes.

She gave him an icy glare, and then tugged on one sock while still managing to hold on. Joe relented and put a calming hand on Rebel's neck, and the horse stilled. The second sock was more difficult since it belonged on the left foot and she had only her left hand free. Joe didn't interfere. He waited and watched until she got so frustrated, she decided to skip wearing the sock on that foot.

"My shoes, if you don't mind," she said, and put out a hand.

"Damn, you're stubborn."

"Me?"

Snorting, he grabbed the sock from her. "It's a little late to be acting all prim and proper," he said, his gaze briefly touching her bare midriff, the hint of resentment on his face startling her.

"I was merely trying to spare you from having to handle my dirty, sweaty socks."

"Oh, for God's sake. Do you know how many times I helped dress Kate when she was a kid?" He slid the sock onto her foot, and then scooped both shoes up with one hand. "And trust me, she wasn't the perfect little lady."

"I'm not your little sister," Lisa said quietly. "And I'm definitely not a kid. Not anymore."

He'd already grasped one of her ankles again, but seemed reluctant suddenly to help her with the shoe. He kept his gaze lowered, cowardly hiding his expression under the brim of his hat. But the gentle way he cupped the heel of her foot, his touch almost a caress, told her more than she suspected he'd like.

"Thank you," she whispered, her words seeming to bring him out of his preoccupation.

He finished the job, and moved back. "No problem," he murmured, his voice low and scratchy, his face still hidden by the hat. "Need help getting down?"

"Please."

He dragged his palms down the front of his jeans, and then grasped her by the waist, just above the belt, his fingers lightly digging into her bare skin. The flesh-on-flesh contact startled her. She'd forgotten that in deference to the heat, she'd tied her blouse up under her breasts. So why hadn't she noticed his warm touch before when he'd placed her in the saddle? Too much commotion? Or had he been more careful to avoid contact?

He did no such thing now. Her pulse quickened as he slowly lowered her to the ground, her body only inches away from his as she made the descent. She was tall, five-eight last time she'd checked, but he was well over six feet, and as her feet found purchase with the ground, she could finally see his features under the brim of his hat.

In his eyes, desire burned like twin torches. The boldness of it stole her breath away. She moistened her suddenly parched lips, drawing his attention to her mouth. Neither of them moved for a long drawn-out minute. With his hands still on her waist, her palms flattened against his chest, they simply stared at each other, her nerves so taut she felt as if she might snap in two.

This was crazy. If he didn't kiss her, she would make the move. Five years was more than long enough to wait. She couldn't stand the suspense another minute. She tilted her head back, dug her fingers lightly into his chest, intent on making her objective clear.

His mouth came down on hers so fast she didn't have time to brace herself. No coaxing, no tenderness, his tongue thrusting inside, fierce and hungry. She sank weakly against him, holding on and kissing him back just as fiercely.

It lasted mere seconds. And then he stiffened, his breathing ragged. He removed her hands from his shoulders, and without giving her another look, swung onto his saddle and rode away.

3

JOE STOOD UNDER the showerhead, face up, eyes closed, and let the cool water rain down on him. He wasn't one to take long showers. Normally he was in a hurry to get to work or fill his belly so that he could catch up on his reading before turning in for the night. But he took it slow this evening. He needed the time and space away from everyone. Away from Lisa.

What was it about the woman that had him wound him up tighter than a rattler about to strike? One look at her yesterday and the tension had coiled inside his gut until the ache got so bad he'd headed to the north pasture, hauling hay and water that didn't need hauling, and nearly pushing himself past his physical limit.

Naturally the men had noticed. Last night in the bunkhouse it had gotten real quiet when he unexpectedly showed up for supper, something he rarely did. Pete had been the only one ballsy enough to call him on it. But one pointed look from Joe and there'd been no more questions.

He stepped away from the spray, opened his eyes and squirted shampoo into his palm. By the time he was done, most of the crowd would have finished eating, some of the picnic tables would have been moved from under the tents to make room for dancing. Most people would be busy talking and listening to the band. Includ-

ing Lisa, he hoped. Maybe no one would notice if he
carried a plate back to the kitchen and ate in peace.

Hell, he wasn't going to have any peace of mind until
that woman was on a plane and away from Texas. Why
the devil had he kissed her? Maybe because he knew
she'd only be here for the weekend. That and the fact
that she wasn't the type who'd expect phone calls and
letters and declarations of undying love. That was the
plain unvarnished truth. Yep, there was something to be
said for sophisticated city types, like a couple of the gals
he knew in Houston. Sex with women like them was
uncomplicated.

Not that he'd planned on going that far with Lisa.
Okay, so the thought had crossed his mind. But only
briefly, and then he'd wised up. Any itches he had could
be scratched in Houston just fine. The fact was, Lisa
scared him. And he didn't know why.

He finished washing his hair, rinsed it and then used
the bar of soap to work up a good lather on his chest
and shoulders. He soaped lower and realized that thinking about her was making him hard. Muttering a curse
did nothing to relieve the mounting pressure. Maybe a
good release was what he needed. He set aside the soap,
took hold of himself and closed his eyes. Sadly, he suspected that he could come three times and he'd still
want her.

"YOU HAVEN'T EATEN yet, either, huh?" Lisa grabbed a
plate behind Joe.

At the sound of her voice, he glanced over his shoulder, his gaze lowering to the paper plate in her hand.
He didn't seem pleased.

"What are you havin', boss?" The big man working
the grill wore a white apron that stretched across his

round belly and looped around his neck. "Ribs, chicken or both."

"Both."

The man grinned. "Good choice. Although I believe I outdone myself on the ribs this year." Using large tongs, he piled the meat on Joe's plate, and then eyed Lisa with a speculative frown that strayed to Joe and back to her. "What can I get you, miss?"

"The same, please." No one else was in line, in fact almost everyone had already eaten. Joe didn't linger but took off for the adjacent table laden with bowls of potato salad, coleslaw and trays of corn bread and biscuits.

Nodding his approval, the cook heaped her plate. Good thing it was one of those heavy-duty kind. "I like a woman with a good appetite." With a nudge of his head and a lowered voice, he asked, "You with the boss?"

Joe's head snapped around. Nothing wrong with his hearing.

She smiled brightly. "Yes, I am."

The look on Joe's face almost made her laugh, but she ignored him, thanked the cook and then moved to join Joe at the buffet table. She'd never admit it, but she'd been stalking the back door of the house, lying in wait for him to exit. He'd taken forever. Much longer than she'd needed to shower, shampoo and apply fresh makeup. If he thought he was going to ignore her the rest of the weekend, he was in for a huge surprise. After that kiss he was not going to ditch her. That would be like giving a dog one lick of a bone and then saying, get lost.

Oh, God, she couldn't go there. Thinking about those few minutes with his body pressed to hers and not being able to act on it would be torture. Talk about an appetizer.

The few moments she took to reminisce was all he'd needed to disappear. She'd scooped up a small mound of potato salad and found herself alone at the buffet. She scanned the remaining picnic tables where a few people lingered but couldn't find him. Out of the corner of her eye, she saw him headed toward the house.

She grabbed some plastic dinnerware and a napkin, and hurried after him. Her good mood had started to slip. His childish avoidance was really starting to annoy her. Especially now that she knew he wasn't as immune to her as he'd pretended. What in heaven's name did he think she was going to do? Force him to have sex with her at gunpoint?

"Joe," she called to him, but behind her the band started off a new set with a rousing country song that pretty much drowned her out.

It didn't matter. She'd probably find him eating in the kitchen and that was fine with her because she'd prefer the privacy. Wasn't that going to make him happy, being cornered like that? The thought cheered her and she picked up the pace.

KATE WAS STILL in the kitchen when Joe sneaked in the back door. His disappointment at not having the place to himself was replaced with concern when he saw his sister dab at her eyes and quickly turn away.

"Hey," she said, opening the stainless steel refrigerator and ducking her head inside as if she were looking for something. "Why aren't you eating outside?"

"They're going to start dancing soon and I didn't want to get in the way. Did you eat yet?" He set his plate on the oak table that had been in their family for a hundred years, and calmly pulled out a chair, his insides on instant alert. Something was wrong. He could tell by the way she rocked back on her heels, a nervous habit she'd developed a month after their parents had died in the car crash.

"I was snacking all day so I'm not hungry." She stood there for a long time, just staring before she finally closed the door without removing anything.

"What's going on, Kate?"

She turned to him with a fake smile, her hands tightly clasped together. "Nothing. Actually, everything went well today. The food was ready on time, in spite of how scattered I've been." She shrugged, the gesture making her look so helpless it broke his heart. "Can I get you something to drink? Tea? Lemonade? A beer?" Her hand went back to the refrigerator door handle.

"What I'd like is for you to sit with me awhile."

"Oh, well, I suppose I could for a minute. Then I want to run upstairs and splash my face. I've been in the kitchen most of the day and I could use some cold water to wake me up."

He nodded. Normally Kate was organized for the annual celebration. She was like a drill sergeant, planning and delegating weeks in advance. Not this year. Joe had chalked up her distraction to her recent engagement but...

It suddenly struck him that he hadn't seen her fiance. Granted, Joe had been busy working yesterday and today but still. "Where's Dennis?"

The stricken look on her face spoke volumes. "I don't— He should—"

The back door opened, and they both turned to see Lisa walk in, balancing a plate of food in one hand. She froze just over the threshold, and tentatively glanced from Joe to Kate.

"Am I interrupting?" she asked, obviously sensing the tension in the room. "I am. I'm sorry."

"No, of course not." Kate stopped her from backing toward the door, taking her by the arm and steering her toward the table. "Your timing is perfect. Joe needs some company while he eats."

The hell he does. Joe grudgingly kept his mouth shut and focused on his plate. There'd be no talk with Kate now. She'd escape upstairs. But clearly her gloomy mood had something to do with her fiance. Maybe it was a simple matter of them having had a fight. Maybe Lisa knew about the problem and could enlighten him. Though he didn't relish talking about his sister behind her back. He'd ask Clint later about what he knew.

The thought appealed. As protective as Joe felt toward Kate, especially after taking on responsibility as her guardian when she was fourteen, he wasn't one to get into deep touchy-feely conversations. He'd always let his brother assume that role, though Clint wasn't exactly Mr. Sensitive all the time, either.

Kate pulled out the chair opposite Joe, and gestured for Lisa to sit. "Would you guys mind if I ran upstairs for a few minutes so I can freshen up?"

Lisa looked helplessly at Joe as she lowered herself onto the chair. He could tell she felt awkward, as if she regretted that she'd intruded. No need for her to feel bad.

"Go ahead," he said with a smile at Kate. "Then come back and have dessert with us."

"Okay." She seemed relieved, already headed for the hall door. "That's a deal."

When she was gone, he transferred his attention to his plate again, and dug his fork into the potato salad. He had the distinct impression that Lisa was staring at him and he glanced up.

Her brows were drawn together in a slight frown. "You smiled."

"Uh, yeah."

"I've never seen you do that before." She seemed genuinely surprised.

He raised a brow. If she was trying to get a rise out of him, it wouldn't work.

She sighed. "That I've seen you do a lot." She stared absently past him, and then her gaze went to the door to the hall. "Something's wrong with Kate."

He paused, mulling over how much he wanted to say. "I know."

Lisa met his eyes. The earnest concern on her face for his sister touched him. "Last night at dinner it was just Kate, Dory, Jessica and me, and we all thought she'd say something about what's bothering her."

"Unfortunately, I don't know anything more than you do."

She studied him thoughtfully. "I haven't met her fiance yet. Do you know him?"

"I've seen him a few times," Joe said carefully. He didn't care for the guy, neither did Clint, and it had been hard for them to keep their mouths shut.

She made a face and distractedly picked up her plastic fork. "I would have felt a lot better if you liked him."

"I didn't say that I didn't."

Frowning, she said, "You didn't have to. Does Kate know how you feel?"

He thought about denying his misgivings, but what was the point? She was a reporter and good at reading people. Besides, she'd obviously made up her mind. "I haven't said anything."

"So she wouldn't be hesitant to tell you if there was a problem."

"I don't know," he said uncomfortably. He'd like to think that Kate felt free to confide in him without fear of judgment. "Depends."

"You know she thinks the world of you."

He shrugged, his comfort level not improving. "Clint and I are all she has." He began attacking his food in earnest, hoping she'd get the hint, quit talking and start eating, too.

"True, you're her family, but her feelings go beyond the accident of genetics. She respects and admires how you took over the ranch and provided for her and Clint."

"Your food is getting cold."

"That's why they invented microwaves. Now, stop being a baby and accept your props."

"Anybody ever tell you you're irritating?"

"Oh, yeah." She started ticking off her fingers. "My boss, my neighbor, the receptionist at work, half my sources and of course, my boyfriend."

He felt as if he'd been sucker punched. He shouldn't have kissed her, although she'd been all too willing.

"No boyfriend." She smiled. "Just wanted to make sure you were listening."

"Make that *very* irritating."

4

SHE LAUGHED, ignored the fork, tore off a piece of chicken and popped it into her mouth. After pensively chewing in silence, she said, "I hope I don't totally bum her out, but I'm going to ask Kate if there's a problem with the engagement." She glanced at him for reassurance but his face remained noncommittal. "If she really doesn't want to talk about it, I'll back off. I don't want to ruin anyone's weekend."

"I have a feeling that since Dennis hasn't shown up, he beat you to it."

"See, this is bad, because I haven't met him, but I'm already not liking him." Lisa stewed over the thought. She'd have to lose the attitude. It wasn't fair to Kate. She gave him a sweet smile. "But of course I'll be on my best behavior when he does arrive."

Joe looked as if he were dying to say something but instead bit into a slice of buttered corn bread.

"And, yes, ye of little faith." She lifted her chin. "I can behave quite well when I put my mind to it."

A slow smile curved his mouth, and she thought her heart would surely stop. This wasn't the smile he'd given Kate. This one was sexy and confident and teasing, and meant especially for her. It totally transformed his face. Made him look younger, not that he was so old, but she liked seeing him laid-back.

In the next instant, he was serious again. "Thanks for being such a good friend to my sister," he said, his quiet sincerity touching her.

"I love Kate," she said. "In school she was the glue that kept us together and in line, kind of like our den mother. God forbid any of us would party too late and miss class." She smiled fondly, remembering the lectures. Good old levelheaded Kate. "Mostly because I travel so much we've only seen each other once since graduation, but we talk and e-mail all the time."

"I know. She's really proud of you."

"She's talked about me? To you?"

He wiped his mouth and hands, and then got up and went to the refrigerator, giving her a terrific view. The jeans he'd changed into were newer, not yet faded, but they fit him nice and snug across his backside. "She mentioned the award you won last year and how hard you'd worked for it. Want a beer or glass of wine?"

"A beer would be great." She watched him pull out two longnecks and then open the cabinet to the left of the sink. "No glass for me."

He closed the cabinet again and brought both bottles to the table. "Going to rough it, huh?"

She liked that he courteously twisted off the cap before handing her the beer. "Don't let anyone tell you that being a reporter is a glamorous job." She licked a speck of barbecue sauce off her finger, and added, "I used to think so until my third assignment when I found out that when you're sent to interview the homeless you'd better be prepared to climb into a cardboard box with them."

His gaze narrowed. "Something tells me you aren't kidding."

"Oh, I assure you I'm not." She lifted her bottle. "To Kate."

"To Kate," he agreed, and raised his bottle in salute.

Lisa took a long sip of the refreshing brew, and then set it aside and picked at her chicken again. "I still can't believe she's getting married. Although of the four of us, it makes sense that she'd be the first one to bite the dust."

Amusement gleamed in his eyes. "Doesn't sound as if you'll be running to the altar anytime soon."

"I'm way too young for that sort of nonsense." She studied him as if seeing him in a new light. He was about thirty-two or thirty-three, and much like Kate in that he was steady, dependable. The kind of man who'd make a great husband and father. "What about you? Have you ever been married?"

He reared his head back as if she'd suggested he commit a grievous crime. "No, ma'am."

"Ever come close?"

"Nope. You?"

"Actually, yes, I did once." She kept a straight face. "I think it was the second grade. Johnny Santini asked so nicely I promised to think about it."

Joe shook his head and went back to finishing his food. "You must have been a real hellion as a teenager."

"Not too bad, considering I was spoiled rotten." She couldn't believe they were having a normal civilized conversation. "My parents had given up hope of getting pregnant when I came along. Mom was already forty, which was considered old for a woman back then."

"You're an only child?"

Lisa nodded. "My father is a cardiologist, although he's retired, and my mother was an attorney who gave up her career when I was about four. They both still live in Chicago."

"They must be proud of you, too."

This was a bit touchy. "They are," she said carefully, "but journalism isn't necessarily a career they would've chosen for me."

"Too gritty?"

"And sometimes dangerous. That's what they think, anyway. It's not true. Most of the stories I follow are quite innocuous."

A patronizing smile tugged at his mouth, not unlike the kind doled out by her parents. "I understand their concern. You're still young and someday—"

"I'm not Kate." That condescending attitude mildly annoyed her when coming from her parents. Coming from Joe it made her want to scream. "I don't need a second father."

He frowned in confusion. "What did I say?"

"You've played the father role so long you don't even get it."

"You're right. I don't." He wiped his mouth and threw down his napkin. "Enlighten me."

"You purposely want to view me as a child."

"Where did that come from?"

She wasn't sure, all she knew was that she'd wanted to wipe that smug "are you sure you know what you're doing" expression off his face. He was using their age difference as a shield. Which was ridiculous because they weren't that far apart. Only in his head. "Do you want to sleep with me?"

Joe stared at her, clearly dumbfounded. "What kind of question is that?"

"You brushed me off five years ago because I was too young, and in retrospect I understand why you did, but no more cat-and-mouse games. You're interested. The kiss told me that much. So what are you going to do about it?"

He pushed his plate aside. "I see you haven't grown out of the spoiled brat stage."

She glared at him. "And you're obviously still a coward."

Shaking his head, Joe scraped back in his chair and picked up his half-finished plate.

"Wait." Lisa gritted her teeth. "I'm sorry. Eat your dinner. I'll shut up."

"That'll be the day," he muttered, and carried his plate to the sink.

"Please, Joe. I know I overreacted. My career is important to me, and I guess I'm touchy about people assuming I'm too young or too inexperienced to take on the meatier assignments." She'd wanted to impress him, show him what she'd made of herself. Because of her looks and her parents' money and social connections, she'd rarely been taken seriously. "I'm really a good reporter," she said feebly.

"I know." He set his plate on the counter. "I read that piece you did on migrant worker abuses."

"You did?"

He tossed his dinner remains in a trash can under the sink. "Yep," he said slowly, somewhat reluctantly, almost as if he'd regretted the admission.

"When?"

His back still to her, he washed his hands and dried them, apparently in no hurry to turn around. "Right after Kate came back from seeing you in Dallas last year."

"Did I give her a copy?" she asked, searching her memory but coming up empty.

He shrugged, clearly uncomfortable. "I think I accidentally ran across the article online."

Her insides quivered with pleasure. The piece had been lengthy, running in a series over the course of three Sunday features. One didn't just happen across something like that unless they had specifically looked it up on Google. She silently cleared her throat. "So, what did you think?"

"That you're one hell of a reporter."

"Thank you. That means a lot." Heat climbed her neck and stung her cheeks. The sensation was totally unexpected and she stared down at her plate, hoping he wouldn't notice. She rarely blushed. What was that about?

"You've hardly touched your food," he said, after an awkward silence. "If you don't like barbecue we probably have something else that—"

"No, this is great." She picked up her fork and speared a chunk of potato salad, amazed at how exposed she suddenly felt. Yet she'd opened the door. Ironic, really, that she'd yearned for his praise and respect, not unlike a child who desperately wanted to please a parent. She glanced at her watch, wondering where Kate was. Was it really seven already? "Oh, no."

"What's wrong?"

She laid down her fork, and used the paper napkin. "I was supposed to e-mail something to my editor an hour ago."

"Is it too late? My office is right off the den if you need to use a computer or phone."

"I have a laptop in my room," she said absently, while checking her phone for messages. "Well, they haven't put out an APB on me yet so there's time." His words finally registered. He'd offered her access to his private office. No way she'd pass up that opportunity.

JOE WISHED he'd kept quiet about having read her stuff. Last thing he needed was to give her the mistaken impression that he'd been following her career. Of course he hadn't. Simple curiosity had steered him toward a couple of articles. That's it. Staring at his messy office, he also wished he'd left his desk in better shape. But he'd just finished doing payroll the day before, and when guests and deliveries had started arriving for the party, he'd let the clutter slide in favor of escaping to the back pasture with the pretense of checking the north fence line for repairs.

"Here, I'll get this out of your way." He reached over to pick up the bulky ledger off his desk and caught a whiff of her tantalizing vanilla scent.

"Don't disturb anything. I'm fine." She ran the tips of two fingers over the antique cherry desk that had belonged to four generations of Mannings. Her hands were nicely manicured, her nails short and clean with a subtle sheen. "This is terrific. How old?"

"Over a hundred and twenty years." He set the ledger on the matching credenza behind them, next to a stack of invoices he needed to review.

"Did someone in your family make it?"

"My great-grandfather." He indicated the credenza with a jerk of his head while pushing aside a cigar box in which he'd tossed miscellaneous receipts. "That was my grandfather's attempt. Not quite the craftsman his father was, but it's serviceable."

She took her time studying the ridged details at the corners and the design etched into the front of the drawers. "You're jaded. This is fabulous."

"I didn't figure you for someone who'd appreciate antiques."

"I like you, don't I?" She smiled sweetly and turned toward the computer.

He decided to ignore the jab. Besides, he had enough on his plate. Like forcing himself to keep his eyes off her perfect heart-shaped fanny as she bent over to press the power button. Her long, slender legs did nothing to curb his imagination, either. Now they were encased in denim, but he remembered well the night of the graduation when the robe had come off and she stood in that short red skirt that barely reached the middle of her thighs.

"I'll give you some privacy," he murmured, hoping he hadn't left out anything on his desk he'd regret, but knowing he should leave.

"No, don't go." She spun around to look at him. "It'll only take me a minute to send the article. I finished it on the plane and I'd planned on doing some nips and tucks before my deadline, but I got distracted. Your fault entirely."

"Right."

"Absolutely it was. If I hadn't had to go riding all over creation looking for you, I would've had plenty of time." She gave him a sassy wink. "Maybe you should make it up to me and proof my article before I send it."

Joe snorted. "What's it about?"

"The importance of multiple orgasms."

5

JOE SHOOK HIS HEAD. She obviously was trying to shock him. Except she seemed pretty damn serious. In fact, she wasn't even looking for a reaction, but instead, sat in his big leather chair and pulled out the keyboard. "Is that a joke?"

"Not to millions of women who believe good sex lasts only five minutes."

"You can't get away with writing something like that in a newspaper."

Lisa smiled. "Wanna bet? Sex is a health issue. They even talk about it on daytime television."

"I'm watching the wrong shows. Or maybe the right ones," he muttered, and she laughed. "Think you'd better find someone else to proof it for you."

"Why? You might learn something." While she focused on logging on, he gazed down at the way the overhead light shone on her hair. The pale color looked natural, even from his vantage point.

With her striking blue eyes, flawless skin, high cheekbones and tall well-proportioned body, he'd bet the ranch that she could easily have been a model. But she'd taken a tougher path and done exceedingly well. Thinking about it now, he knew she'd chosen the perfect field. She struck him as a woman who thrived on challenge, who thrilled to the chase, and apparently that had included him.

That part he didn't get at all. They could hardly be more different. Was that the appeal for her? Or was her motive simply that he'd turned her down?

The computer was slow. He'd been meaning to order another one. But she didn't complain, just settled back in the chair as she waited for her information to appear on the screen. She glanced around the room, her gaze resting on the built-in oak bookcase that dominated the far wall.

He'd collected hundreds of books over the years, both fiction and non, the latter mainly pertaining to ranching or animal husbandry. He'd even kept a few of his college textbooks. Not that he deluded himself about ever returning to school.

"Are those all yours?" she asked, squinting to make out the titles.

"Most of them. Some belonged to my father. He liked Louis L'Amour and Larry McMurtry's Lonesome Dove series."

"Have you read them?"

"When I was younger."

Her e-mail screen popped up and she went to work, her fingers flying over the keyboard at impressive speed. "Sorry," she said. "This won't take long."

Not wanting to hover, he hooked his thumbs into his back pockets, and strolled over to the bookcase to idly peruse book spines. He envied her command of the keyboard. How many times had he told himself he'd order one of those typing tutorials? He'd never learned the skill in school, having selected science classes whenever he'd been given the choice.

Clint was the one who'd been more business oriented. He'd even earned a business degree from the University of Texas. And although he shared the office duties with Joe, Clint was more their PR man, schmooz-ing with customers, getting top dollar for their beef and always managing to buy low.

"Okay, done," she said. "Should I shut down the computer, or did you want to check e-mail first?"

Joe smiled. "Is it that time of the year already?"

"Ah, you're one of those." She powered off. "Some-times even I find computers to be necessary evils. But in the long run, it does make my job easier. I'm very familiar with the Delete key." She joined him at the bookcase. "I have to admit I've never read Louis L'Amour, but I love the Lonesome Dove series."

She stood close, her shoulder brushing his arm as she studied the assorted titles. Then she bent lower, her hair falling forward, the wispy edges caressing her cheek.

His gaze followed the curve of her spine down to the flare of her hips, to the tempting mound of her bottom. He breathed in deeply, and forced his attention back to the books, willing the mounting heat in his groin to cool down.

"You've saved your textbooks," she said. "Eew, my least favorite subjects, science and biology." She slanted him a coy look. "Don't tell me you were one of those geeky boys in high school."

"Sweetheart, I played football for three years in high school and a year and a half in college. I was not a geek."

"Excuse me," Lisa said, laughing. "But why all the college science courses?"

"I wanted to be a veterinarian."

"Really?" She straightened, with a surprised lift of her brows. "That's a lot of schooling, right?"

"It would've taken another four years after college."

"Whoa, as bad as regular medical school."

"Yep, but interesting."

"So says you." She made a face. "I could barely pass basic science class. They lost me with frog dissection. The idea gave me nightmares for weeks."

"Then good thing you deal with words."

She tilted her head to the side, and thoughtfully studied him. "Have you ever considered going back?"

"To school?" The idea startled him. Maybe once he had, right after Clint had graduated, but then there was Kate, who had been accepted to the school back East, and the ranch had grown almost busier than he could handle.

"Your credits would still be good, or maybe not after ten years." She frowned. "I don't know what the cutoff is but it wouldn't matter. I bet you'd nail most of your core credits by exam and could skip the classes."

He sighed. "I'm not going back to school at this point."

"Why not?"

"In case you haven't noticed, I have a two-thousand-acre ranch to run."

"Yeah, but you have Clint and I bet half the ranch hands you have working for you have been here forever. How much supervision do they need?"

"And you know all about the Sugarloaf how?"

It was Lisa's turn to give him a patronizing smile he didn't much care for. "Okay, if you need an excuse, I'm sure you've got dozens of them," she said blithely and turned back to checking out the books.

There she went, being irritating again. Probably just as well. They'd been getting too chummy when he should've been maintaining his distance. Time for him to go back outside and socialize. "To the far right there are four shelves with books on tape, if you're interested. A lot of them are current."

"I love listening to books read aloud." She turned back to him. "But since I'm only going to be here one more day. And two nights," she added, moving closer and using the tip of her finger to trace his lower lip. "I can think of far more appealing things to do with my time."

LISA COULD TELL he didn't know what to do with her. If she thought he really wasn't interested, she'd leave the poor guy alone. But he'd given her enough signals to tell her otherwise, and she had no intention of wasting another minute.

Without moving a muscle, his eyes hooded, he gazed down at her. "Are you always this much of a tease?"

"Don't kid yourself." She lightly scraped her teeth along his jaw. "I'm not teasing."

"Why not Clint?" he asked, his voice lower this time. "He's not shy with the ladies. If you'd given him the go, he would've been all over you."

She smiled. Clint was damn fine, maybe even better looking than Joe. He was the kind that knew it, too, though he seemed like a good guy. But Joe…there was just something about him that was earthy and sexy yet incorruptibly decent… "You saying you're shy with the ladies, cowboy?"

"No."

"Or just not interested in me?" She trailed her finger to the seam of his lips.

He hesitated, with a subtle lift of his chin. "No."

"No, that's not what you're saying…" She wouldn't make it easy for him. Why should she? He was the one acting like a child. "Or no, you're not interested."

"You know darn well I'd be lying if I claimed I wasn't interested," he admitted hoarsely.

"That's right. I would know." She leaned into him, feeling the hardness of his arousal pressed against her belly. "For the record, I'm not interested in your brother. Never have been, never will be. I want you."

"You're a very persistent woman," he murmured, the tension in his upper body starting to ease.

"I am. Get over it."

One side of his mouth lifted in a slight smile. "Pushy, too."

"Tell me something I don't know." She took his hand and put it on her waist.

He didn't wait for her to orchestrate the next move. With his other hand, he cupped the side of her jaw, stroked her cheek with the pad of his thumb. "You are so damn beautiful."

The earnestness in his eyes made her knees weak. She'd heard those words before, from other men, many of them sincere, but they'd never had the same heady effect on her as they had at this moment.

"But pushy," she reminded him, the lameness of her joke bringing a flicker of amusement to his face. Did he know how off balance he'd thrown her, how much her confidence had slipped?

He nudged her chin up and kissed the side of her mouth. And then he kissed the other side while sliding his fingers into her hair. He grabbed a fistful, and then let go and watched as the strands fell down past her shoulders.

"Don't ever cut it," he whispered.

"I'd be willing to make a trade for that promise."

His eyes came back to hers, and again he touched her flushed face, then trailed his fingers down her neck, the front of her blouse, over the swell of her breast. He'd barely touched her, yet already she felt as if she were coming apart at the seams.

"Go back to the party, Lisa."

"Not a chance."

"You realize someone could walk in," he said, his eyes fixed on her lips.

"Let them."

Smiling crookedly, he fingered her nipple through her blouse, drawing a circular pattern until it was hard and aching. She wanted his mouth on her, wanted to see him without his shirt. Wanted to see him naked, period. But he was right. This wasn't the place.

"Think anyone would miss us if we went to my room?" To further persuade him, she cupped a hand over his fly, pleased when he tensed and hissed. He was rock hard, and she probably needed to only push a little to get her way.

"What do you think?" He briefly closed his eyes, and moved against her palm.

"That I don't really care."

"You would later." Joe shifted so that she couldn't exert any more pressure. "What if Kate's fiance shows up and she can't find you?"

Lisa groaned at the unfairness of his argument. He was right, though, damn it. "Then I guess we'll just have to make out here for a few more minutes."

He smiled and gently moved her hand away from his fly. "There are laws against torture in this country."

"You mean, I can't strip you naked, tie you up and suck you like a lollypop?"

His mouth opened in shock, and then produced a startled laugh.

She grinned. "Sorry. Couldn't resist."

He yanked the hem of her blouse from her jeans and slid a hand up her bare belly to her breast. The thin, lacy bra was a flimsy barrier for his determined fingers. "Yeah, I know what you mean."

She moaned, arching her back slightly when he rolled her nipple between his thumb and forefinger. "You rat."

He dipped his head, and his mouth caught hers in a wet hungry kiss that stole her breath and forced her to clutch his shoulders for support. He backed her up against the bookcase, his blatant need almost a physical thing that thickened the air around them. She brought her leg up to rub him intimately, and he groaned into her mouth.

"This is crazy," he murmured raggedly. "We have to stop."

"I know," she agreed, and with one hard jerk, unsnapped the top half of his shirt.

His skin was smooth and taut over hard muscle, and she shivered with the pleasure of running her palm up his chest, and then back down to his belt buckle. His muscles contracted, allowing enough room for her to slide her fingertips beneath the waistband of his jeans.

"Lisa—" Her name was still on his lips when she heard the doorknob turn. The door opened before they could part.

"I saw the light on and figured—" Kate's voice died.

Mortified, Lisa briefly squeezed her eyes shut. When she opened them, they met Joe's. He looked as if he'd just received a death sentence.

6

ONLY MIDMORNING and it was already so stinkin' hot, Joe's T-shirt clung damply to his back. Working in the line shack this time of day wasn't the smartest move with no trees to shade the old place, but the roof had sprung another leak and he was determined to fix it before the next rain.

After having lain in bed awake for an hour, restless and irritable, he'd gotten dressed and headed to the stables earlier than usual. Originally, he'd planned on taking today off, just as he did every year. The rodeo started around one and took up most of the day. The picnic and fireworks that followed would wrap up the weekend's festivities, and tomorrow everything would be back to normal. That is, after Lisa got her pretty little ass off the ranch.

Shit, he couldn't even think about her without seeing Kate's shocked face. Last night had been a disaster, and totally senseless. He'd known better than to act like a horny, brainless teenage boy, right there in his office, the door unlocked. No one ever knocked. It wouldn't occur to them that the door was closed because he wanted privacy. That's just the way it was around the place.

To Kate's credit, she'd been cool about catching him pawing one of her best friends. She'd promptly closed the door and let them pull themselves together. In fact, by the time they left the office, she'd already gone outside to join the party. Later, she'd even made a joke about it when she saw him sneaking off to his room early, tired of forcing smiles and making small talk, but he'd been in no mood for humor. He'd felt too much like a damn fool. Six hours of fitful sleep hadn't changed a thing.

He had no idea what Lisa did the rest of the night. He figured she'd ended up on the dance floor, but he'd stayed clear of the area. Although she'd seemed pretty shaken after Kate had walked in on them. She'd just tucked in her blouse, pushed a hand through her tousled hair, and with her chin up, walked out the door without uttering a single word. Amazing, now that he thought about it…the not talking part.

One of the boards he tried to pry loose wouldn't give, and it didn't help that he had to approach it from an awkward angle. He reached up, using the claw end of the hammer. Sweat trickled into his eyes, stinging like hell. He lifted his other arm and swiped his forehead, knocking his hat off in the process.

He wasn't one to cuss much, but he let out a string of curses that would've made the ranch hands take notice. Last night was his fault. This whole mess with Lisa was his fault. He'd had no business responding to her, no matter how much she'd taunted him. No matter how much he'd wanted to touch her hair, feel the softness of her skin, to taste her. What sane man wouldn't want her? But he was tougher than that. He'd always prided himself for his willpower.

Joe scooped up his hat and hung it on the end of the curtain rod. His gaze caught on the faded pink curtains that Kate had made for her junior-year home economics' project. Clint had tried to tell her there was no place for curtains in a line shack, but she'd been incensed over being forced to study something as sexist as Home Economics. She'd asked Joe to go to bat for her with the school principal, and he'd refused. One of the few times he'd refused her anything, but he'd been overwhelmed with his duties at the time and hadn't seen the point.

Furious with him, she'd taken the class, made the curtains and declared they would stay up until they fell off. A few years later, with age and wisdom, he knew he'd failed her by not going to the principal in her defense. Last night, he'd failed her again.

He opened his canteen and took a swig of water, frowning when he thought he heard something. Listening for a few seconds, he recognized the pounding of horse's hooves galloping toward the shack. Only Clint knew where he was. Had something gone wrong at the rodeo? An injury?

Joe capped the canteen, and grabbed his hat, glancing at his watch on his way out the door. Only eleven. The rodeo hadn't started yet. That was a relief. He went around to the side of the shack, squinting in the direction of the approaching rider, and immediately saw the tangle of pale blond hair floating on the breeze behind her.

Gritting his teeth, he had a good mind to mount Rebel and outrun her. But he wouldn't do that to either horse. Instead, he waited impatiently the few seconds it took her to reach him.

"I can't believe you," she said before bringing Selma to a stop. "What are you, twelve?"

He leaned against the shack wall and folded his arms across his chest. Man, was he going to kick Clint's ass. "What are you doing out here?"

She swung awkwardly out of the saddle, found a

post and secured the reins. "Joe Manning, you have to be the most stubborn man I have ever met."

"You rode all the way out here to tell me that."

"Yes, and I shouldn't have had to. Why are you hiding out here like a child and not going to the rodeo?" She stood a couple of feet in front of him, her hands bracketing her hips.

Her jeans rode low, the waistband resting below her waist, while the hem of her stretchy blue top stopped an inch short of the denim, exposing her navel and a tempting strip of tanned skin.

He tried like the devil not to stare.

"Kate told me you never miss the rodeo," Lisa said accusingly.

"I'm sure my sister had a lot to say."

"As a matter of fact, she did. She loves the idea of the two of us together. She hopes we get married, and give her lots of nieces and nephews."

Joe's jaw slackened, his mouth hung open, but damned if he could think of a thing to say.

"I'm kidding." She growled with frustration. "Kate doesn't care that we were tickling each other's tonsils. I doubt she'd care if I were to sneak into your room tonight." She threw up her hands. "Nobody cares, Joe. Only you."

He pushed away from the rough shack wall, not knowing if he should shake her or kiss her. "You tell me you weren't embarrassed last night when she walked in."

"Well, of course I was. I'm not an exhibitionist, nor did I want to upset Kate, which I promise you we did not." She gave him a small smile. "But that doesn't mean I'm going to let the incident ruin the time we have left."

"*We* have left? Thought you came to see Kate."

She sent him a stony glare. "Don't."

Joe lifted his hat off his head and resettled it, then pulled the brim low, irritated with himself for trying to make her feel guilty. The woman sure could bring out the worst in him. "You find out what was wrong with her last night?"

"Her fiancé was being a jackass. Called at the last minute to say he couldn't come until today." Lisa's brows drew together in a concerned frown, and she wrapped her arms around herself. "I feel badly because I haven't met the guy yet and now I've officially decided I don't like him."

Joe shook his head. "Kate can do better," he murmured, unthinkingly, and then got annoyed with himself again. He had no right voicing his negative opinion about Kate's future husband. Especially not to her friend. "I'd appreciate you not repeating that."

"Of course I won't." She thoughtfully nibbled her lower lip. "She doesn't seem happy. If I'd finally found someone I wanted to spend the rest of my life with and made the decision to do the whole wedding thing, I'd be delirious. I'd be—" She glanced sheepishly at him. "Marriage is a big deal."

Watching the pretty flush steal across her cheeks did something funny to his insides. She was tough and bold and plain speaking most of the time, but this glimpse of her softer side was surprisingly unsettling. He cleared his throat. "So he's coming today for sure."

She shrugged. "So he says."

Joe rubbed the back of his neck. Kate would probably kill him, but he had a good mind to have a word with the guy.

"Don't you dare say anything to him," Lisa said, her gaze narrowed in warning. "It's none of your business."

He had no idea how she knew what he was thinking,

and he didn't like it. But she'd uncrossed her arms, and his attention quickly switched to the way the stretchy top clung to her breasts. His body reacted, and he had to move.

"I have about an hour's worth of work," he said turning away from her. "And then I'll head back."

She caught his hand, waited until he met her eyes, and said, "I'll wait."

"Don't trust me?"

"Do I look stupid?"

"You—" He sighed. "You look beautiful."

She blinked, slackened her hold on his hand. "Stop it."

Joe smiled. Improbable as it was, he had a feeling he'd embarrassed her. "Stop what?"

"Saying things like that. You're just trying to shut me up."

He touched her cheek. His palms were smudged and grimy. He had no business putting his hands on her. "I know better. A whole stampede of cattle wouldn't shut you up."

Her mouth curved in a sweet smile. "That's probably true."

He lowered his hand. She squeezed the other one tighter, but he tugged it away. "I'm a filthy mess."

"I'm a bit sticky from riding out here myself. Maybe we should take a shower." She paused, running a palm up his chest. "Together."

"Where do you propose we do that?" Just thinking about seeing her wet and naked made him spring to life again.

"Don't you have a bathroom inside here?"

No way he'd take her inside the shack with its loose floorboards, rough unfinished walls and dingy appliances. The place was okay for him and the boys to hole up in when the weather was bad or they'd been working past dark, but it wasn't fit for a lady. What amazed him was that she was willing to consider stepping inside the place. "There's a bathroom, but not a very good one. It's probably older than you."

"Is it clean?"

"Yeah, it's clean."

"That's all I ask."

He shook his head. "Not here, Lisa."

Her eyes lit up. "That sounds promising. I wasn't flat-out rejected."

He tried not to think about her hand still rubbing his chest, or the way her lips were shaped in a perfect bow. "Has any man ever told you no?"

She blinked, looking offended, as she absently traced his left nipple. "You're my first. Not to turn me down, but the first man I've ever chased. It's very humbling, I must say."

He couldn't take the tension a second longer and grabbed her wrist. Again it surprised him how small-boned she was and he adjusted his grip. "You can stop that now."

"Ah, sensitive, huh?" Her lips lifted in a satisfied smile.

His normally unresponsive nipple wasn't the only thing getting hard. A few inches closer, and she'd find that out. He sucked in a breath, and shifted closer to the wall, trying to put some distance between them, but she moved with him. She was crazy. He couldn't imagine how ripe he smelled. She hadn't escaped the humidity, either. A damp sheen coated her cheeks, but that enticing vanilla scent still clung to her.

She titled her head back, her warm gaze searching

his face, touching his mouth and telling him that if he
didn't kiss her, she'd do the honors.

"You pick the dumbest times to—" Something suddenly occurred to him. The little vixen. She knew she
was safe out here at this dilapidated old shack with
minimum facilities. Just like yesterday afternoon at the
stream. Last night in his study with over a hundred
people just outside. She always came on to him when
she thought he couldn't act on her seduction.

She twisted her hand free and placed it over his
pounding heart. "To what?"

"Aren't you the clever one?"

She frowned prettily. "What do you mean?"

He picked up her hand, kissed the back and released
it. Then he smiled. "You really are a tease, after all."

Her eyes widened. "How so?"

"You like the thrill of the chase. The catching part
isn't so much fun, huh?"

She drew back. "Where did *that* come from?"

He sighed. "Come on. You've consistently chosen
the most inopportune times for us to get down to business. Sweetheart, around here, we call that catch and
release."

"That is not—" Her words fell off, her lips still
parted as if she couldn't think of what to say next. "I
can understand why you think that's what's been going
on, but that is so not the case."

"Right."

She glared through narrowed eyes, and then checked
her watch. "You have an hour and a half to ride back,
take a shower and get ready for me. Twelve-thirty. I'll
meet you in your room." She jabbed a finger in his
chest. "Mister, you'd better be on time."

WELL, SO MUCH FOR FOREPLAY.

The entire thirty-minute ride back to the ranch, Lisa had bounced between annoyance and frustration. He was dead wrong. But he obviously believed that she'd been toying with him or else he'd know he didn't have to play her to get her into bed. Had she subconsciously teased him? No. A series of coincidences as far as her timing, that's all it was. They had limited opportunities to be alone, coupled with the problem of a gazillion people milling around the ranch.

She went light reapplying her makeup and then stared into the bathroom mirror. Her hair was still damp even though she'd taken a blow-dryer to it, but so what? She planned on it getting good and messed up. She just wished the much-anticipated event had sprung up more organically rather than her ordering him to be standing at attention at the appointed hour.

She let out a heartfelt sigh, and grabbed the peach-colored halter top she'd hung on the door hook. After pulling it on, she adjusted the built-in bra, bending forward as she tweaked the cups to allow for maximum cleavage. The only clean thong she had was pink and her capris were white, but she doubted that would matter to Joe. She finished dressing while contemplating how she'd find his bedroom.

It was upstairs, she knew; all the family's bedrooms were on the second floor while the guest rooms were located downstairs. There wasn't a snowball's chance she'd ask Kate, even though she doubted her friend would care, and anyway, everyone was already at the rodeo. Which would ultimately work to Lisa's advantage, because if she had to, she could knock at each bedroom door until he answered. Assuming he'd decided to comply with the command performance. The memory of her romantic edict made her wince.

A quick check of her watch, three squirts of her favorite vanilla scent, and then she fluffed her hair and left the room. The house seemed eerily quiet, though she could hear faint applause and shouting coming from outside as she ascended the stairs. At the top, two doors had been left open, both rooms empty. She continued down the hall, stopping at the first closed door and knocking softly.

The one behind her opened, and startled, she put a hand to her throat. She spun around to face Joe. He wore clean jeans but no shirt. His muscled chest was gloriously smooth, his hair still damp, and his feet bare. He gave her a slow smile that could melt her stoic Russian grandmother's heart.

"I forgot to ask you which room was yours." Astonishingly, she found she was somewhat tongue-tied and quite a bit nervous.

"I just got out of the shower but I was listening for you." He stepped back, looking totally at ease, as if he'd invited her in for tea. "It took me longer than I thought to wrap up at the line shack and then I ran into Kate outside."

She walked through the door, her gaze darting to the big four-poster king-size bed, the royal-blue comforter already turned back. "Did she ask why you weren't at the rodeo?"

He shrugged a shoulder. "I told her you made me a better offer."

"Shut up."

Joe grinned. "She was looking for you, so my guess is she's done the math by now. You can still change your mind and go to the rodeo."

She hadn't missed the glint of challenge in his eyes, and lifted her chin in response. "Hell, no."

He closed the door behind them, the soft click of the lock engaging sending the blood roaring to her ears. "I brought up a bottle of wine and a couple of beers, if you're interested," he said, his voice coming from just over her shoulder.

"Thanks. Maybe later." She didn't dare turn around, not yet. "This room is huge. Is it the master?"

"Nope. We've left my parents' room virtually untouched. But all of the upstairs' rooms are big. There's even a balcony through those French doors if you want to catch some of the rodeo."

She caught the humor in his voice and was tempted to call his bluff, but she wasn't that foolish. "Sure, while we're at it, we can wave to Kate and your brother."

He pressed a kiss to the side of her neck, his deep rumbling laugh vibrating against her skin and sending a shiver of delight down her spine. "You look really nice," he whispered.

She dropped her chin, hoping he'd find that sensitive spot at the top of her spine. "So do you."

He lightly bit her. Right there. Right where she wanted it. Gripping her upper arms, he moved his mouth to the side, closer to her ear. "I'm glad you showed up."

"You seriously had doubts?" She tried to face him, but he held her firmly in place.

"I did." His tongue forged a path across her bare shoulder. He stopped to nibble and taste, before dragging his hot mouth down her shoulder blade. For an instant, she thought she felt him at her nape, a slight tug on the bow holding up her halter top. But then he turned his attention to the other shoulder blade, dusting featherlike kisses down her heated skin.

She stared at the framed photograph of a white stallion on the far wall, unable to move, not just because he was holding her in place, but because she was afraid. Her body had gone limp, her knees almost useless to keep her upright. The exquisite feeling of his touch while she was unable to watch what he might do next was, she imagined, like being blindfolded and tortured. Not the painful kind of torture, of course, but agonizing in its own way.

Tension tightened her chest, twisted deep in her belly, buzzed along her nerve endings. She realized she'd been biting down on her lip, and feared she may have drawn blood. Forcing herself to breathe evenly, she moved her shoulders, hoping he'd let her go, praying he wouldn't.

He loosened his grip, but before she could decide if that was what she wanted, he slid his arms around her, banding her against his chest. His skin was fever hot against the bareness of her back, his breath cool as he nuzzled her neck. With his arms crossed in front of her, he found her breasts, gently cupping their weight in each of his big rough palms.

She moaned his name, and reached behind to touch him. There wasn't room to squeeze her hand between their bodies. His arousal was pressed tight against her bottom, so tight she could feel every twitch of his cock and it was driving her crazy. She wanted to see him, all of him and wrap her fingers around the silky hardness she knew she'd find.

"Joe." Her low throaty voice sounded as if it belonged to someone else. "Let me go."

He froze for an instant, his arms tensing and then immediately released her. "Did I hurt you?"

"No." She spun to face him. "Definitely, no." She touched his freshly shaved chin and breathed in his clean male scent. "It feels good. But I don't know that I can stay on my feet much longer." When confusion flickered in his face, she added, "You make my knees weak, cowboy."

His nostrils flared slightly. His hooded gaze riveted to her lips. With a hooked finger, he lifted her chin and kissed her tenderly on the mouth, and then scooped her into his arms. She let out a surprised shriek, and then covered her mouth, though too late to stifle the noise.

He smiled. "No one is going to hear us. I promise you that," he assured her as he carried her to the bed.

Stopping at the side where the comforter had been partially turned down, he had to shift her weight so that he could finish the job. The impracticality of him carrying her and trying to ready the bed, made her giggle. He looked down at her with a single raised brow.

"You're so cute when you're being gallant, but I can stand at least long enough to crawl between the sheets."

"Well, there goes my puffed-up ego." He kissed her forehead and set her on her feet.

She lingered, stroking her hand down the muscled contours of his chest. "Ah, and very nicely puffed it is." She pushed her hand lower and rubbed his fly. "And I wasn't talking about your chest."

He grunted, arching back in escape. Challenge darkened his face, his mouth curved in a warning smile. "Remember when I said no one can hear you?"

"Uh-oh. Beware the sleeping tiger." She dived across the bed, but he caught her ankle.

"That's right, sweetheart." He dragged her back, and then straddled her, his thighs pinning her hips while he found the ties to her halter.

WITH ONE HAND Joe leisurely untied her top, and with the other he brushed a lock of hair away from her flushed face. Her blue eyes were bright and alive and full of daring. That his hand shook slightly didn't surprise him. Ironic that she'd referred to him as the sleeping tiger. Lisa was like this exotically wild creature that seemed cute and cuddly and tame one minute, and then feral, dangerous and impossible to handle the next. He'd never met another woman like her.

He only hoped one taste of her forbidden fruit wouldn't ruin him for life. Stoke an addiction that would destroy his chance for a more permanent relationship. He needed a nice reliable woman who'd enjoy living on a ranch and bearing his children. Although he hadn't thought about marriage much, he knew that at his age he should be considering prospects if he wanted to start a family before he was too old to appreciate throwing a football with his sons.

But Lisa made him think of the other side of the coin. The strong physical connection he ached for, as well. From the moment Kate had told him Lisa was coming to the ranch, he'd wrestled with forcing away the all-consuming thoughts of her. Over the last two weeks, she'd popped into his head at the damnedest times. What was it going to be like after they'd made love? Would he forever be comparing other women to her?

"Need help with something?" she asked. Amusement tinged with impatience gleamed in her eyes.

"You are the mouthiest woman I've ever met." He leaned down and bit her lower lip.

"Hey." She bit him back, harder than he'd nipped her, and pinched his ass.

"You asked for it." He yanked the top from her body.

"Are you kidding?" she said, laughing. "I'm practically begging."

He scarcely heard her teasing, but stared down at her bared breasts, so ready, so perfect. She was right. Her distended nipples begged for his eager tongue. He lowered his mouth and drew her in, using his teeth and tongue to elicit a raspy moan. His desire to go slow vanished, and as he laved her breasts, he unbuttoned her waistband. She took care of the zipper, then wriggled her hips as she pushed the white fabric down her thighs.

She kicked off the capris, unsnapping his jeans at the same time. He stopped her then because he was so hard that getting the zipper down without doing damage was going to be tricky. When he drew back to take over the task, he saw that she was left with only a scrappy triangle of pink silk at the tops of her smooth toned thighs. Her belly was flat with a hint of muscle, just enough to make her femininely taut.

His heart raced with anticipation, and he hurried to get his jeans off. He flung them toward the walk-in closet's open door, not caring when they hit the wall and fell to the floor in a heap.

Lisa's laugh sounded slightly nervous. "I just thought of something. I don't have any condoms with me. I hope you do, or else we're screwed."

"Actually, neither of us would get screwed," he said, "but luckily I'm prepared."

She laughed again, this time a deep, throaty laugh that alone could have turned him on. "Very naughty, Mr. Manning. I like a man who surprises me." Her gaze went to his tented navy blue boxers. "I just knew you wore boxers, but I thought they'd be white."

He smiled and twisted around to get the small, unopened box out of the nightstand. He didn't know why he kept them there because he rarely invited women to the house, at least not to his room. His extracurricular activities were always kept separate. Oddly, he liked having Lisa here. It felt right to have her sharing his bed. It also felt a hell of a lot like trouble.

8

WHILE HE OPENED THE BOX, she got up on one elbow and casually reached over to run her hand over his hard-on. He tensed, giving her a warning look that she blithely ignored. She wanted those boxers off. Right now. But she wanted to make sure they had a condom ready, too. She wasn't in the mood to take it slow. Maybe later after the emergency was over, and she'd got him out of her system. Maybe even tonight after everyone had gone home and they weren't expected to socialize. She didn't have to leave for the airport until noon tomorrow, and if she were persuasive enough, maybe she could keep him in bed until midmorning.

Knowing she'd be leaving in a matter of twenty-four hours, she realized the weekend suddenly seemed to have flown by. Already she knew she'd miss Joe, and the irrational thought that she should delay her flight by a day unsettled her. It was impossible of course. Too much work awaited her.

She consoled herself by hooking her fingers into the elastic waistband of his boxers and drawing it down low enough to free his thick, glistening cock. He grunted in surprise and tossed the box aside. She scooted closer, her pulse racing as she circled her fingers around him, squeezing lightly and watching his face contort with both agony and pleasure. He finished the job of getting rid of the boxers, and then stretched out beside her. He found her bare breasts, and the rough texture of his work-hardened fingers against her sensitive skin felt unexpectedly erotic.

"Give me the condom," she whispered, briefly closing her eyes and arching upward.

"Why the hurry?"

"I admire your restraint. Really, I do. Now, give me the damn condom."

Joe smiled, and did as requested. Then he grabbed a couple of pillows and bunched them behind his head and watched as she used the tip of her finger to spread the beaded moisture over the crown of his penis. He hissed when she wrapped her fingers around him and slowly drew her hand down to the base. She stroked her way back up before sheathing him.

He slid his hand between her thighs, gliding over the dampness of her flesh and dipping into that slick, wet crevice that was ready and waiting for him. Homing in on her clit, he rubbed in a tight steady circle, using the perfect amount of pressure to bring her close to the edge.

She knew it wouldn't take long to come, and she wanted him inside of her when she did. Quickly, she moved to straddle him, holding her breath as she lowered herself over him, feeling him enter her slowly, and then slide deeper and deeper inside her until she was a quivering mass of nerves.

Barely missing a beat, he moved with her, finding her clit again, and with his other hand, gently kneading her breast. She closed her eyes as delicious sensations shimmered through her body, building in intensity and bringing her to the brink of mindlessness until she started to convulse and whimper. She crumpled against him, and he lifted her up, then pressed her back to the mattress.

In seconds he was over her, pulling her legs around his hips as he pushed into her. The gentleness was gone, and he slammed fast and hard, demanding yet giving, his mouth on hers, his tongue mimicking the rhythm of his thrusts. Trembling with need, she hung on to him, afraid she'd fall into the abyss if she didn't. She came again, a moment before his raw cry shattered the silence. He strained against her, his taut biceps quivering as he kept his weight from crushing her.

"Lisa," he moaned hoarsely. He thrust again, a second time, and then a third before collapsing on her.

She noticed that she'd been digging her nails into his shoulder and she relaxed her grip. She shuddered with an aftershock, and he reached up to push the hair off her damp cheek.

"Am I too heavy?" he asked near her ear.

"Don't you dare move." Sighing, she slid her arms around his back and hugged him tightly.

He kissed her shoulder. "I was worried after all this time it might be anticlimactic."

She grinned. "I did, too."

"So what's the verdict?"

"Fishing for a compliment?"

"Yep."

She slid her hands down his back and squeezed his ass. "You were amazing."

"Glad I hit the mark. When do we get to do it again?"

She laughed softly, feeling carefree and as light as a feather. No, she did not want to leave tomorrow. "If you're up for round two, cowboy, I'm game."

He rolled over onto his back, a slow sexy smile curving his mouth. "Well, sweetheart, you're going to have to give me a minute or two."

"One." She curled up alongside him, her questing

hand rubbing his belly, the contentment she felt truly remarkable. For her, afterglow was normally fleeting. After the main event, she usually got antsy. She was more like a guy that way. "That's all you get."

"Spend the night with me," he said, and pressed a kiss to her temple.

His words surprised her, because subconsciously she'd already made that assumption. It didn't seem as if they'd just made love for the first time. There had been no awkwardness between them, no tentative touches. In fact, the familiarity of their intimacy was almost scary. "You just try and keep me away."

"I was hoping you'd say that," he whispered huskily, and with a start, she figured out that he'd been uncertain about where they stood.

"Don't get too freaked out, but I was trying to think of a way to stay an extra day," she admitted, his pleased smile making her feel like crap. "But I can't."

He nodded, clearly disappointed. "We'll have to make the most of tonight." He pulled her closer. "After the picnic supper and fireworks everyone disappears fast to be ready for work tomorrow. We won't have to socialize long."

"Good, especially since we already had our fireworks." She hid a smile. "You're really not bad for an old guy."

His left eyebrow went up, and he tickled under her ribs. "An old guy?"

She squirmed, laughing. "How do you lift one brow like that at will? I'm so jealous."

"How can you smell so good all the time?" He inhaled deeply and stroked her hair. "You smell like vanilla even when you've been out riding."

"Ah, that's a trade secret." She paused, thinking

about how much easier and fun riding had been this morning. Yesterday, she'd been convinced she'd end up breaking her neck. "Teach me how to ride better."

This time he hesitated, drawing back to look at her, a myriad of questions reflected in his eyes. Questions she wasn't sure she could answer. "We don't have much time for riding lessons," he said slowly.

"No, I guess not." She swallowed, ordering herself not to be impulsive. Making promises she couldn't keep would hurt them both. "I vote we get dressed and make a cameo appearance outside. Then we can sneak back in until the picnic."

"Very devious." He kissed her briefly and withdrew his arm. "I like it."

She forced a smile, and scooted to the edge of the bed. This was horrible. She missed him already.

FOR AN HOUR, Joe grudgingly played host, going through the motions, catching up with neighbors and lamenting the retirement of the community's local hero, champion bareback rider, Ben Anderson. For the past ten years, he'd been the main attraction at the small rodeo, which otherwise was kept low-key, staying away from the more dangerous events and sticking with saddle bronc riding, barrel racing, steer wrestling and roping, and this year for the first time, the calf scramble. That had been Kate's idea because she knew everyone would be disappointed that Ben wouldn't be riding.

Until five minutes ago, Lisa had been in Joe's sights as she talked with Kate and Dory, one of the other two women who came with Lisa for the weekend, and with whom Clint appeared to be quite chummy. That was a shocker. Joe obviously *had* been out of touch the past two days. But right now he was more concerned about where Lisa had gone. Had she returned to the house? Had he missed his cue? Bad enough he'd been listening with only one ear while Dwayne Goodwin had complained about his exorbitant feed bill last month.

"Hey, cowboy." She'd come up from behind him, the mere sound of her voice a balm to his spirit.

"Well, howdy, ma'am." He touched the brim of his hat and winked. "I was just wondering where you'd run off to."

She smiled slyly, then transferred her attention to Dwayne and introduced herself. The nosy old codger was all eyes and ears, and if Lisa let him, he'd pelt her with questions until next Sunday.

"See you later, Dwayne." Joe slid an arm around her and steered her toward the refreshment booth, well aware that by tomorrow morning half the county would be buzzing over the mystery woman Joe Manning had been cozying up to.

"You do realize that everyone is staring," Lisa said.

"Yep." He kissed her cheek, longing to plunder her mouth, but figuring his neighbors had had enough of a shock for one afternoon. Had any of them actually seen him with a woman in the last ten years? He couldn't re-call. Out of the corner of his eye, he saw Clint staring, too. "Want a beer?"

"I want you," she stated, her warm breath drifting over his skin, her vanilla scent wiping away all common sense.

"Let's go." He lowered his arm and took her hand.

"Where?"

"To bed."

"Wait." She put on the brakes and tugged at his hand. Keeping her gaze level with his, in a low voice she said, "I don't think you understand how many people are watching us right now."

"Do you care?"

Her eyes sparkled with wonder and excitement. "No, but—"

He hauled her against him and kissed her hard, stopping short of using his tongue. Reluctantly, he released her. "I figured we'd spell it out for them." He smiled. "Just in case there was any doubt."

"You're crazy."

"I know." He couldn't argue that. Tomorrow he might kick himself in the rear end, but right now he'd never felt more alive in his life. "Ready?"

"For just about anything," she said, smiling happily, and this time she took the lead, dragging him toward the kitchen door. "It's going to be really embarrassing later at the picnic and fireworks."

He chuckled. "Don't sound so cheerful about it."

"I'm just saying…"

As soon as they made it through the door, Lisa spun toward him, wrapped her arms around his neck and nearly knocked him over with her enthusiastic kiss.

He hoped he wasn't about to blow it, but something had been bugging him for the last hour. "Look, were you serious about learning how to ride?"

"No," she said, regret chasing the light from her eyes as she lowered her arms and tightly clasped her hands together.

His heart plummeted. How foolish he'd been to think she wanted to see him again. He shrugged. "No problem."

"It was an excuse." She slumped, looking miserable. "I'm the coward. I was afraid to—" She squared her shoulders. "I have a story to cover in Tulsa next month.

It should only take a few hours. Meet me there. Spend the weekend with me."

Joe smiled, his chest tightening. "Any time, any place." He gathered her in his arms and showed her how much he meant it.

Epilogue

HALFWAY THROUGH the picnic supper on Sunday, Kate's concern over her fiance's absence had turned to anger. By the time Dennis finally showed up, thirty minutes before the fireworks, she'd descended into such a funk she could hardly force a smile. How long ago had she asked him to keep the weekend free? Two months? Three months? Oh, he had an excuse for not showing up sooner. He always did.

When school was in session, she'd understood his busy schedule. She even appreciated his ambition to be the next assistant superintendent of their school district. Who knew how many dinners and fund-raisers she'd attended with him because he claimed it was important that he keep a high profile, and be involved in the community. But when was it her turn to have some of his attention?

She watched him chat up Melvin Bradshaw and his wife, Marilyn. Figures Dennis would home in on the richest cattleman this side of Houston. His ranch was the only one larger and more profitable than the Sugarloaf. Undoubtedly he was a powerful man to have in one's corner.

An awful thought suddenly occurred to her. Was that the appeal she held for Dennis? Her family's money? Their influence in the community? No, she was exhausted and being paranoid. He'd simply been late, for heaven's sake.

Two days late, damn him.

She forced her resentment aside and scanned the crowd, looking for Lisa. She hadn't met Dennis yet. Dory and Jessica both had been introduced to him when he first arrived. Dory had just been confiding that she and Clint had made plans for him to visit her in Hawaii for a week. It was kind of sweet, really, how Dory had seemed to be asking for Kate's blessing.

She would never admit it to Dory or her brother, but seeing the two of them together had been a shock. They were so different, Dory so earthy and Clint an irrepressible charmer, not at all a match she personally would have tried to arrange. But they looked so cute together she felt guilty for the sharp pang of jealousy she'd experienced. Did Dennis ever look at her the way Clint gazed admiringly at Dory?

And then there was Ben and Jessica. Another surprise. She saw them sitting on a blanket on the grass by the tent, apart from the crowd, Ben's arm around Jess, pulling her close. While everyone ogled the fireworks' display lighting up the sky, they had eyes only for each other. Kate had learned that they also had made plans to hook up in a couple of weeks. That was saying something, since Kate knew how insanely busy Jessica was at the magazine.

Kate saw Dennis shake Melvin's hand and then step away from the Bradshaws. He glanced around, and she lifted a hand to let him know where she was. Dennis spotted her, waved, and then moved on to talk to the Thompsons, who owned the well-known Red Rock Ranch.

A wave of sadness swept over her. Oddly, she'd never

felt so alone in her life. She turned away, desperately wanting to disappear into the shadows. That's when she saw Lisa. She was with Joe, standing on the second-floor balcony off his room, watching the fireworks. His arms were wrapped around her as she leaned back against his chest. Kate sighed at the picture they made. She truly hoped something wonderful came of this for them. Joe deserved the happiness. If anyone could bring him to life, Lisa could.

To her horror, Kate found herself blinking back tears. She was getting married in six months. She should be ecstatic. Not feeling as if she were about to make the biggest mistake of her life.

Afraid someone would see her sniffling, she backed toward the house. She had to go inside and pull herself together before the fireworks were over.

She made it to the kitchen door, but something stopped her, a force so strong it was as if someone had physically blocked her path. Slowly she turned around. Standing in the driveway, under the red glow of the fireworks she saw the silhouette of a man. His stance seemed familiar. He almost looked like…

Her heart all but stopped.

What was Mitch Colter doing back in town?

* * * * *

Harlequin® A *Romance* FOR EVERY MOOD™

PASSION

For a spicier, decidedly hotter read—
these are your destinations for romance!

Silhouette Desire®

Passionate and provocative stories
featuring rich, powerful heroes and
scandalous family sagas.

Harlequin® Blaze™

Fun, flirtatious and steamy books
that tell it like it is, inside and outside
the bedroom.

Kimani™ Romance

Sexy and entertaining love stories
with true-to-life African-American
characters who heat up the pages
with romance and passion.

Look for these and many other Harlequin and Silhouette
romance books wherever books are sold, including most
bookstores, supermarkets, drugstores and discount stores.

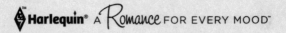

Harlequin® A *Romance* FOR EVERY MOOD™

HEART & HOME

Heartwarming romances where love can
happen right when you least expect it.

Harlequin® American Romance®

Lively stories about homes, families
and communities like the ones you know.
This is romance the all-American way!

Silhouette® Special Edition

A woman in her world—living and loving.
Celebrating the magic of creating a family
and developing romantic relationships.

Harlequin® Superromance®

Unexpected, exciting and emotional
stories about life and falling in love.

Look for these and many other Harlequin and Silhouette
romance books wherever books are sold, including most
bookstores, supermarkets, drugstores and discount stores.